# INTRUSION

## Theresa M. Odom-Surgick

*Intrusion* Copyright © 2013 by Theresa M. Odom-Surgick

Cover created by: Donna Osborn Clark at

CreationbyDonna.com

Interior design and typesetting by: interiorbookdesigns.com

Editing Services by: ColPer Research, Inc. (Harolyn Hood & Susan Perkins)

Jamaican Translations by: Terri-Ann Gordon and Thelma Gordon

Published by:

DMO Music & Creative Arts Publishing

ISBN 978-0-615-94452-4

# INTRODUCTION

The Merriam-Webster Dictionary describes an *intrusion* as the act of intruding or the state of being intruded; especially: the act of wrongfully entering upon, seizing, or taking possession of the property of another.

Intrusions come in all forms. Whether mentally, physically or emotionally, there are things in life that can cause them to take place in different ways. Your focus on the *intrusion* will take you away from the real issues of life. It may be for a short moment or for as long as a season in time.

This book, *Intrusion*, in its fictional form is filled with many examples of intrusions that we might face on a day-to-day basis. How many intrusions can you find within this writing? You just have to open your mind to view them. There is always, well generally, a way to escape from the control of the intrusion—you will see what I mean as you read this book I entitled *Intrusion*.

# CHAPTER 1
## Beginnings

A ttorney Jovan Wilkins sat in his office at 2304 River Street, preparing for another day of work at his newly formed law practice. Sitting at his cherry wood, executive L-shaped desk, he began making a checklist for himself. Rolling a ballpoint pen between his fingers, his work was briefly interrupted as he sadly thought of his dad, Jerald A. Wilkins, a former prominent lawyer in the upstate New York area.

His dad was now retired and in a nursing home suffering with Alzheimer's disease. Following his dad into the practice of law was a major step. Interning for several years propelled him and it gave him the experience he needed. Graduation day was a proud one for Jovan, as his dad was able to see him walk across the stage and receive his degree. Seeing his one and only son graduate and pass the bar exam, which followed their great family tradition of law enforcement, was always his hope and dream. Jovan reminisced about this, thinking how blessed he was that it happened before all was lost in the annals of his dad's memory because of his disease.

In the quietness of his small but comfortable office, he picked up his cup of hot black coffee—no sugar or cream—and sipped as he thought about the good times with his dad. Hearing the chimes of an old clock hanging on the paneled wall brought him back to reality and the business at hand. *It's time to refocus*, he thought. *It's time for me to get back down to business.* So he finished his checklist, mulling over the things that he had listed. Even though his practice was new, he still had a steady flow of clients—some of which were grandfathered to him from his dad. The business was bringing in a substantial income. Soon he would be able to hire a full-time staff and this excited him. Things had gotten a little hectic and he needed a break from being the one who was taking on the task of preparing important documents and marketing for new clients.

His first order of business lay before him in a manila folder. As he thumbed through a ten-page document, he wrote down numbers on a yellow scratch pad and prepared to make his first call of the day.

"Let me get started before this day gets away from me," he said aloud.

Picking up his phone, he began dialing the first number on his list. While he waited for an answer, he took another sip of coffee and then just as he cleared his throat, he heard "Hello."

Responding, Jovan said, "Hello. May I please speak with Pastor Joseph Freeman?"

"This is he. May I ask with whom I'm speaking?"

"Yes, Pastor Freeman. This is Attorney Jovan Wilkins of Wilkins Law Group. I'm calling on behalf of one of your parishioners, Ms. Rachel Vandelyn."

"Little Jovan? Is this Jerald Wilkins' son?" Pastor Freeman asked with a jovial voice.

"Yes it is, sir."

"Oh my goodness!! Well, I'm sure you're no longer little. Your dad and I were college roommates."

"Yes, Pastor Freeman. He told me about some of your college days."

Frowning, he said, "Hope he didn't tell you too much, son."

"No, sir. It was all good. He really admired and looked up to you."

"Really? Well, thank you. Glad to know it. Now you said you're calling on behalf of Ms. Vandelyn?"

"Yes, sir."

"Rachel is one of our most respected parishioners here at Empire Christian Community Church. In fact, her family is some of our founding members. How may I help you, Mr. Wilkins?"

Before answering, he adjusted himself in an old wooden, rickety desk chair that creaked with every move. He refused to get rid of this piece of furniture that at one time belonged to his dad. It helped to keep him reminded of his goal in life: he wants to be successful like his dad.

Once he was comfortable, he replied, "I'm calling because Ms. Vandelyn recently acquired the estate of her aunt, Ms. Myra Vandelyn, who suddenly passed away. As executor of her estate, she has asked that we contact you to request your presence at the reading of the will."

"I'm aware that Ms. Myra, passed away; I performed the interment ceremony. We are greatly saddened and miss her strong presence here in our congregation." A questioning expression that showed in the wrinkles forming on the Pastor's face, displayed his concern as to why he was being asked to attend.

He then asked, "Attorney Wilkins, may I ask you a question?"

"Yes, Pastor Freeman."

"Why does Rachel want me to attend this reading? Although I am more than willing to take part, I need some answers before I can give you my availability."

"I understand, sir. This has been very hard for her. The struggle has taxed her physically, emotionally, and mentally. Rachel would like you there for your spiritual support."

"Oh my, I wish she had called to let me know what she's been going through. I talked to her at the funeral service and visited with her a few times at the house. I had no idea — she seemed alright. You can count on me to be there. Rachel is a valued member and we loved Ms.

Myra. So whatever I can do to support her is important to me. Just tell me when and where you need me. I'm a very busy pastor, but I'll move my schedule around to make myself available."

Making a check mark next to Pastor Freeman's name, Jovan said, "Thank you, sir. The reading is this coming Wednesday at 12 noon in the Dendell Conference House on River Rock Road in Clinton, NY. I apologize for the short notice — is the day and time convenient?"

"No need for an apology. Hmm...let me see," he said, as he flipped through the pages of his planner to find the date. My secretary is out today, but, according to my schedule, it should be fine. Do you think I'll be able to leave by three o'clock? Our mid-week bible session begins at 7pm and I need some time to make final preparations for my lesson."

"No problem, sir...it will take no longer than an hour."

"Great! Now, one more thing before we end this call. I usually bring along one of our intercessors when I go out to any consultation. Will that be okay?"

"I don't see it as being a problem, Pastor Freeman. Just give me the person's name."

"Mother Hattie Larkin."

Quickly writing her name down, he said, "Okay. I just added her to the list. I'll see both of you on Wednesday. Thank you for your time, sir."

"Jovan, I would be remiss if I didn't make this statement. It would also be good to see you back in church. Do you hear me, Son?"

"Pastor Freeman, I—"

"Just think about it, okay."

"I will, sir. Goodbye."

"Good day, Mr. Wilkins."

As Pastor Freeman hung up the phone, he said a quick prayer. "Dear God, please let things run smoothly. Let your presence change not only the atmosphere, but let it change the hearts of your suffering people. In Jesus' name; Amen."

# CHAPTER 2
## Questions

"Anita, I'll be so glad when all these legal matters are over. Poor old Auntie suffered so much and it was hard seeing her lie in that bed in the state she was in. I couldn't stand it any longer."

Cupping her face in her hands, she tearfully said, "I'm so sorry, Aunt Myra, but I had to do it. I just had to."

Rachel's personal assistant, Anita, was always attentive to her needs and said, "Here's a tissue, Rachel. Now what are you talking about? What did you have to do?"

"I had to let her go. Even though a DNR was signed and in place, the doctor asked me what I wanted to do and I gave them permission."

"Permission? Permission to do what?" Anita asked nervously.

"To stop any kind of measures to save her. Once her heart stopped that was it. I had to let her go! It was so hard turning her life over to them. When they showed me that piece of paper, I knew it was the best thing to do but I really struggled with it. My hand was shaking uncontrollably and I dropped that DNR to the floor. When it was done, I felt at peace. But right now, I'm questioning whether or not I should have allowed it to go through. Maybe I should have fought more for her right to live. That should have been God's decision—not Aunt Myra's or mine."

"Rachel, why do you continually go over and over this same issue? We've talked about this so many times before. You didn't do anything wrong. You act like you've committed murder. You can't keep beating up on yourself. Ms. Myra signed that paper and would not have wanted to continue living like that and you know it. You have to start praising God for the life that He blessed her to live. Now she's at peace, resting in His arms. She's in a better place."

"A better place?" Rachel said bitterly.

"Yes, a better place, Rachel."

"Why do people always say that! A better place? She should be here with me!"

"Rachel, get a hold of yourself."

With a balled fist placed on her forehead, gently tapping her head, Rachel said, "I know. I know, but it's so hard to imagine what the next few days and weeks are going to be like without her here with me. Anita, my beloved Aunt Myra is gone. She's gone!"

"Come on, Rachel. You can't stop living your life because she's gone. She wouldn't want that for you."

"But Anita, I'm still struggling with the fact of not knowing the details of what happened to her. We had such a beautiful day together. She was good when I left the house and then for me to suddenly receive a call saying she's in a coma in the hospital? Dear God! It's still hard to believe that this is even true. I need to know what happened to her."

Anita took Rachel and embraced her tightly, knowing that this was a hard thing for her. Myra Vandelyn was unable to have children and raised Rachel and her brother, Devin, as her own. Rachel's extreme analytical mind was tearing her up inside. With her head resting on Anita's shoulder, she said through tears, "How did this happen? Things are so gray and I can't get over the fact that she is now dead and missing from my life. I need some clear understanding in order to get over this loss."

Pulling away from Anita, Rachel said, "You called the paramedics. What happened? How did you find her?"

This was the first time that Rachel ever asked for the facts of what had happened and, deep inside, Anita was getting a little frustrated with Rachel as she thought, *Uh oh...It's going to take her a while to get over this one, especially when I tell her about Devin. God, please give me the patience and love to deal with her. I really don't have time for this, so I need your grace to handle it and now!*

"Rachel, I wasn't the one who called. I didn't find her. It was your brother, Devin."

"Devin?"

"All I can do is repeat what he said."

"What did he say, Anita?"

At first hesitating to give Rachel the details, she asked, "Do you really want to hear this?"

"Yes, I do. Tell me...I need to know."

Breathing deeply, she went and sat on a black, leather stool near an artist's drawing board in the office. Adjusting the seat and leaning with her elbow on the board, she said, "Okay, Devin said that he found her on the floor unconscious. He tried to wake her, thinking she had just fainted. He even said he got some ammonia cleanser from under the sink, and put some on a towel to see if that would help to wake her."

"What?"

"Yeah...guess that has worked in some cases. When she didn't come to, he called the police and paramedics."

Rachel stood there with hands on her hips, listening intensely. She tried to fathom what she was hearing and was still in disbelief.

"I can't...I just can't accept this the way it is."

Anita sucked her teeth.

Seeing her frustration, Rachel threw up her hands and said, "Well, there has to be something more to it. What was Devin doing in the house anyway? I know for a fact that Aunt Myra took the keys away from him a few months ago."

Realizing the value of this statement, Anita said, "Hmm...you're so right. How did he get into the house when he didn't have keys?"

"Anita, something is not right with this. He had robbed her one too many times and she was fed up with his thievery. How did he get in here? Nothing is adding up. What's he hiding? Anita, please get him over here, now!! I need to talk with Devin and get to the bottom of whatever he's not saying. Get him over here now!"

# CHAPTER 3

## Devin's Subtle Remorse

T he one love of Devin's life was something he thought always made him feel good — alcohol. He had a strong desire and daily relationship with vodka on the rocks. As he sat in his favorite chair, he hugged a cup of the clear, cold liquid between his warm hands. Sadly, he thought about the very last argument he had with his Aunt Myra a few weeks before her death.

*Quietly turning his key in the lock, he peeked in and called out, "Aunt Myra? Are you home? Aunt Myra!" When he got no response, he walked in gently closing the door. Devin was always looking for something when he visited his aunt. He grew up an angry young man and did not know how to give. What he couldn't get, he took without a thought or care about how it would affect others. In Yiddish terms, Devin was what you would call a schnorrer...one who habitually takes advantage of others' generosity, often through an air of entitlement.*

*His aunt did her best to raise him and Rachel after the abandonment of their parents. This took a toll on Devin, who was eight at the time. The pain and hurt he felt bled out on the way he acted and treated others; especially his sister, Rachel. There was no gratitude for the love that his aunt tried giving, so his anger drove them apart.*

*Again he called out, "Aunt Myra! You here?" Still, he got no answer. Looking around, he found his aunt's purse sitting open on the mahogany buffet in the dining room.*

*Hmm… her purse is here. She must be out for a walk, he thought while picking it up and perusing it. He dug deep down to the bottom, pulling out her personal items. He laid unopened envelopes, mints, gum, and a makeup bag on the buffet and kept digging until he found what he was looking for — her wallet. He then threw everything else back into the large, black purse and opened the wallet.*

*I really need a few bucks. She won't mind if I take a couple of dollars. A fifty…she's got a few in here. I doubt if she'll miss it. I'll take one and return it later. He unzipped his jacket and pulled out his billfold. Before he could put the money and the wallet away, Aunt Myra appeared and yelled, "Devin! What are you doing? Give me back my wallet and my money, you thief!"*

*Her sudden appearance and voice coming out of nowhere startled Devin who jumped and yelled, "Aunt Myra!" She snatched the wallet and the money out of his hand and pulled her purse out of his reach.*

"You didn't have to snatch it, Auntie. I called, but you didn't answer me."

"I was in the shower, but that doesn't give you the right to go through my purse and take my money. I'm tired of you sneaking around and taking anything and everything you want. This is going to stop today. Give me your keys to the house."

For years, she had put up with Devin and his undesirable ways. It had come to this point in time where she could no longer handle him and the added stress he placed in her life.

"But Aunt Myra, you can't do that! I was going to give the money back when I get paid next week."

"That's not the point, Devin. It's a matter of principle. You went through my bag without my permission and took money out of my wallet. Now give me the keys! Since you want to be a thief, I'll treat you like one and keep my door locked to your sticky fingers. Enough is enough! I've had it with your stealing!" Anger was raging in Aunt Myra. Usually a soft-spoken person, the level and tone of her voice threw Devin off for a moment as he thought of what to say. He knew that she was now at the end of her rope with him and this was the beginning of the end of this type of behavior in her home.

"So it's going to be like that? You're going to keep me locked out of the house and make me ring the bell or knock on the door to get in like a complete stranger?"

"If that's what I have to do to keep you from stealing from me, then yes. Give me the keys you crook!"

*Devin was so angry. With squinted eyes and pierced lips, he said, "Here! They're yours! Catch them if you can!"He threw the keys at her, hitting her on the arm, which later left a bruise. She yelled in pain at him as the keys fell to the floor and slid under the buffet.*

*Devin turned and walked away as she said, "Devin Aaron Vandelyn, you come back here and get these keys right now! I mean it! Right now!"*

*He kept walking and said, "No, Aunt Myra. You've had it with me and I've had it with you. Don't worry about me coming back. Get the keys yourself!"*

Now she was dead. Sitting here in the loneliness of his small apartment, Devin was battling the demons that had set up camp in his mind sending daily reminders of that volatile conversation.

His cup of vodka was no longer cold in the cradle of his hands as he took a long warm sip, trying to kill the pain of what he said to his aunt on that cool spring day.

The phone rang, startling him. He let it ring a few more times before answering.

"Hello?"

"Hello, Devin?"

"Yeah. Who's this?"

"This is Anita."

"Anita who?" Devin already knew who it was, but would not let on. This was his evil way of making sure he was always in control of any situation.

"Devin, knock it off. This is Anita...Anita Gonzalez, Rachel's assistant."

"Yeah...and what do you want?"

"Rachel needs for you to come to the house right away."

"Oh really? What for? And why couldn't she call and ask me herself?"

"Devin, just get over here right away? She needs to speak with you now—it's a matter of utmost importance."

"Utmost importance? Well I—"

"Just get here within the hour, please. Thank you. Goodbye!" Anita hung up on Devin.

"Why that—Arghh! What can Rachel possibly want from me?...sitting up in that house like she's so important. Why couldn't she just call me herself? She doesn't run me; I'm a grown man. She can't tell me what to do. I'll show her a thing or two—just like when we were kids. Stupid broad."

# CHAPTER 4

## Devin Is Confronted

D ing dong.

"I'll get it...must be Devin."

"Thanks, Anita."

Opening the door, she said, "Hello Devin. Please come in. Would you like some coffee or tea?"

"You got something stronger?"

"No...I'm afraid not."

"Thanks but no thanks, and when did things get so formal around here?" Looking across the room, Devin shouted, "Rach, I'm home!!"

"Please, there's no need for this. And things around here haven't changed. You've just been so intoxicated at times that you just weren't cognizant of it."

"Hey! Now watch what you say and how you say it! Who made you judge over me? Have a little sympathy; I'm grieving too. She was my aunt as well. Be a little easy on me."

Glaring at him, she said, "Humph... I apologize."

"Now…that's better," he arrogantly said.

"I'll get Rachel for you. She's waiting in the—"

Before she could get the words out, Devin pushed his way past Anita, and said, "Oh that's okay. I know my way around."

She tried to get past him, but making it a game of chase, Devin ran and went into the den before Anita got there. When he entered, Rachel was looking out the window gazing in deep thought.

Devin and Rachel's history was one of hidden secrets, an unhealthy relationship, and violent scenarios. Grabbing her around the waist, something he knew not to do, set off a volatile response in Rachel.

Tearing away from him, she said, "Don't touch me! Never again! We've been through this before. Don't ever put your dirty, filthy hands on me!"

Anita rushed in and said, "I'm sorry, Rachel, he pushed his way through. Do you need my help?"

"No. I'm okay."

Turning to Anita, Devin said, "And what exactly do you think you can do, Anita?"

With anger-filled eyes, Rachel said, "Don't you ever touch me again! Believe me. You know what happened before. I'm not afraid to handle my business again—I'll do what I have to to protect myself. I'm not the scared little girl I once was."

Stepping back, holding his hands up in surrender, Devin said, "Hey...cool it. Don't act so excited to see me, sis!"

"How am I supposed to act? You've caused us so much grief and pain. You tell me how I'm expected to act?"

For once in his life, Devin was speechless and didn't say a word as she continued with her ranting.

"You stole from Aunt Myra like some common thief even after all she did for you. She was a mother to us and raised us as her own, which she didn't have to do, Devin! You remember how it was...not knowing where our dad was and then having to deal with our own alcoholic mother not wanting to raise us."

Rachel stood there with her hands on her hips and moved up close to Devin and said, "You wasted Aunt Myra's hard earned money for a college education that you just took and vomited away with all of your drunken binges. You're lucky you even graduated. Did you really love her? Or did you just use her to get everything you wanted?"

"Wait a minute!" Devin yelled.

"No...you wait! Look at this scenario, Devin. What have you gained from all your years of stealing and deception? Now your well water is all dried up and what do you have to show for these years of her support? You have nothing — not one thing. Aunt Myra is gone — what

are you going to do now? What will you do, Devin?"
Rachel said with her finger pointing in his face.

Devin stood there with an evil smirk on his face and
let her continue, but in his mind, he thought, *I'll let her
say her little speech, but it won't happen again…never again.*
Tightly grabbing her pointed finger in his hand, he
sternly said, "Get your hand out of my face."

Rachel quickly pulled away from him and taking a
step back, she angrily said, "Don't you dare look to me to
help you. I'm not giving it! My hands are clean and I'm
not going to get them dirty with your nasty mess
anymore…I'm done! You better believe that I am finished
with you!"

Devin was tempted to retaliate, but thought better
and contained the anger that was brewing deep inside
and said, "You think you're so smart. Don't you, Rachel?
I'm well aware of my issues so you don't have to
pinpoint each one of them with a sticky note. I loved her
too."

Shaking her head in disgust she said, "Oh did you?
Did you really?"

At this point, anger was like a red hot poker burning
as sweat dripped down Devin's forehead and into his
eyes. Deep within, he knew that Rachel was right, but he
didn't have the will to give into her.

"Did you really love her, Devin? I want to know," she
said, continuing to press him for an answer.

"Yes, I did. Whether you want to believe me or not, I did. I just expressed it somewhat different than you. And how do you know the well is all dried up? What about her will? I know she must have left a little something in it for me. There has to be something!"

Rachel turned her back to Devin and said, "You know what, Devin? You're so repugnant. And to top it off, you're a crazy, lying, thieving, ludicrous man. I don't like you. Pastor Freeman says that I have to love you and I'm trying to because you're my brother, but it's too hard. Argh!! I just can't do it!"

Rachel sat down on the sofa. Things had gotten out of hand. It was time to cool down. Nothing more would be settled with yelling and tearing each other apart. A moment of complete silence filled the room as both of them began to calm down.

Devin broke that silence and softly said, "Why did you have me come over if you were just going to rip me apart? Why, sis?"

The calm was short lived as the old, nasty attitude of Devin's reappeared and said, "Oh, did you need a little friendly comfort, sis? You know I can do that real good!"

Rachel almost lost it again, but with as much restraint as she could possibly grasp hold to, looked up at him and calmly said, "What is it with you? You don't have a clue as to how you ruined my life, do you? You disgust me, Devin. I've kept your dirty little secret for years."

"Don't you mean *our* dirty little secret? Sis?

Rearing back, Rachel looked at him and said with intense, "I hate you so much, Devin. I've learned to deal with everything that you did to me through counseling. I'm not going to ever let you hurt me again. Before I do that, I swear with my whole heart, I'll kill you. Just try me."

Acting as if he had a whip in his hand, he said, "Whoa...whoa, little horsey! Let's not get violent here. Besides, you know you enjoyed it."

Rachel had enough of his arrogant, nasty behavior and quickly jumped up from the sofa and slapped Devin in his face. He grabbed her hand and held it so tight that she thought he would break her bones as the searing pain rushed through her hand and up into the tips of her fingers. Trying to pull away, she almost lost her balance as tears welled up in her eyes. He stood there holding tightly and acted as if he enjoyed seeing her in pain. He finally let go.

Rachel stumbled backwards and massaging her hand, she sat back down on the sofa and tearfully said, "You're so lucky I don't have a gun in my hand right now, Devin! I swear I would shoot you dead right where you stand!"

With a smirk on his face, he said, "Wouldn't you just like to. But you wouldn't. You love me too much," he said with sarcasm, licking his lips.

"Ugh! Ooh! I hate you so much."

Standing up and walking away from him, she bitterly said, "Before you leave out of this house and I mean for good, I want you to tell me about the day you found Aunt Myra. I want every detail."

"What happened? I already gave that information to the cops. She's dead and buried and I don't have to tell you a thing!"

Turning and facing him, she wiped the tears from her eyes and said, "Oh yes you will. You'll tell me everything right now. I have the right to know. Tell me, Devin—I need to know!"

"Okay sis, settle down.  I'll tell you just to get you off my back and stop your acting as if a crime's been committed. Geez!"

Devin sat down on a small ottoman near the sofa and said, "When I got here, I found her sprawled on the floor, next to the stairs unconscious. I called the cops and they called paramedics. I tried to wake her...gave a little mouth to mouth and even tried the old ammonia trick. That didn't work, so I waited till the paramedics showed. That's it. That's all I know."

He got up and walked over to the window, and stood there blowing his hot breath on a single pane and then doodled a design with his pointer figure on the fogged up glass.

"There's more...isn't there, Devin. Why are you turning away from me? I can always tell when you're lying. Can't you look me in the eyes and tell me everything you know? There has to be more to it than that. Please don't hide anything from me. What else is there? How did you even get into the house?"

"Oh..." he said stopping in the middle of his drawing.

"Oh...yes, I know that Aunt Myra took the keys from you. So how did you get into the house, Devin?"

Turning and facing his sister, Devin said, "Duh...I had an extra set of keys."

"Why you—Oohhh." His brazen sarcasm was wearing her thin.

"Be nice, Rachel, or I'll leave and won't say another word about this," said Devin with eyes stretched wide open and looking threateningly at Rachel.

"Okay...okay, Devin. Just tell me!"

"That's better, sis. Now where was I? Hmm. Oh—I used my duplicate key to get into the house. I didn't know she was here. She usually goes to that old church ladies meeting on Tuesdays and I thought she would be there and not here in the house. I was hungry, so I went to the fridge to get something to eat. There weren't any leftovers, so I made myself a couple of scrambled eggs with cheese, toast and bacon. I sat down and ate...drank my coffee and when I was getting ready to leave I walked into the room and there she was. Poor thing...I tried to wake her thinking that she had just passed out. I tried getting her to sniff the ammonia. When she wouldn't wake up, that's when I waited for the paramedics. There's nothing more to this story. That's it."

"So you sat down and ate while poor Auntie lay on the hard, cold, wooden floor? You just found her lying there after you satisfied your greedy gut!"

"Yes...just found her there. Wait one minute. Are you trying to accuse me of something, Rachel? Just what are you implying?"

"I'm not trying to accuse you of anything. I'm just trying to get some clarity. The last time I saw her she was fine. I just can't understand what happened. I haven't been able to rest and I won't until I find out."

Devin drew so close to Rachel's face that she could feel the heat of his body next to hers and smell more than a whiff of his alcoholic breath as he angrily said, "Well you understand this one thing and get it straight in that weak little mind of yours! I didn't do anything! You got it! I did nothing!"

With those last angry spatting of words, Devin pushed his way past Rachel almost knocking her down, rushed out and slammed the door shut as he left the house. With tears streaming down her face, she watched him leave through the bay window and speed off into the night in his gray Buick Century.

# CHAPTER 5

## Under Investigation

A few days passed after Rachel's confrontation with Devin, but she still could not shake the feeling that Devin was being deceitful. Taking matters a little further, she called her friend, Attorney Jovan Wilkins, to get a recommendation for a good private investigator who came to her home right away.

"Rachel…Detective Danison is here to see you."

"Thanks, Anita. Please bring him right in."

As she waited for him to be escorted into the living room, Rachel stood there thinking, *I'm so glad he's here. I really want to get to the bottom of this. Something is just not right.*

"Ms. Vandelyn…so nice to meet you."

Standing before her was a handsome, blond-haired, 5'10", awesomely built man. Looking into his bright, gray-blue eyes, Rachel tried to hold in a gasp that almost escaped her lips as he placed his hand in hers to greet.

She quickly tried to contain herself and said, "Thank you…thank you for taking the time to stop by, Detective Danison," she spoke with a slight stutter of words. "I—I guess it's great to have friends like Jovan Wilkins and contacts within the police department. Please have a seat."

As they walked over to the sofa and sat down, he said, "Yes, Attorney Wilkins and I have been friends from childhood."

Rachel had to force concentration in order to hear what he was saying. His voice was rich, deep and silky, almost melting her with every word he spoke.

"We both started out with the police department, but Jovan went his way to law school and I stayed with the police. We've had our battles, toughed it out and he's even set me up with a few blind dates. This isn't a set up—is it?"

"Oh no, Detective," Rachel said blushing. "I can assure you that this is not a set up for a blind date."

In her mind, she was wishing otherwise, but had to remember that this was all about business. It was time to get some real questions answered.

"Oh…okay. Don't get me wrong…I wouldn't mind it at all," he said looking into her eyes. "I just don't like the element of surprise that my friend has thrown my way on one or two occasions."

*Me too, Detective…me too*, she thought.

He then pulled out a small notepad and pen and asked, "So how can I help you, Ms. Vandelyn?"

"First, please call me Rachel, Detective. We don't have to be so formal. Do we?"

"No, not at all, Rachel."

"Now...would you like a little something to drink— coffee, tea or water? I think we also have some fresh, ice cold lemonade in the fridge, if you'd like."

"No thanks. I'm good. So—," he said as he opened the notepad.

"Alright, well the reason I called you here is because, as I'm sure Jovan has told you, my aunt suddenly passed away recently. The circumstances of her death seem so strange and unbelievable to me. The day she died, I was with her hours before. We were together most of the day. We went to the mall, did a little shopping, had lunch and sat talking in the park for a good while. She was healthy. Even for her age, Aunt Myra could probably run a marathon if she really wanted to. There was nothing wrong with her."

"How old was she?"

"A young sixty years old and she didn't look her age, I might add," said Rachel with pride.

"Hmm...well did you have an autopsy performed on her body?"

Dropping her head and shaking it, Rachel said, "I'm afraid not."

"And why not?"

Defensively, Rachel said, "Is it necessary? Aunt Myra was a very private person and always made a big deal about not having an autopsy when she died. She didn't want anyone messing over her body and thought that something like that didn't have to take place—it's just too personal, so I didn't have one done."

"Hmm," he said as he laid the pad and pen on the table.

"Well, Rachel, I hate to be the bearer of bad news, but in order to go any further with this investigation, we're going to have to exhume her body and perform an autopsy to see if there is anything suspicious. I know you want to adhere to your aunt's wishes, but that's the only way we can go. Do I have your permission to start with the arrangements?"

"Detective, that really is the only way?"

"Sorry, but it is."

Rachel's mind was now filled with even more anguished turmoil. She sat there wringing her hands nervously at the thought of what she was about to do. She wanted to grant her aunt's wish and felt that she would be out of order if she did anything else. *First that stupid DNR and now this*, she thought as a warfare erupted in her mind. Detective Danison could see how agitated she was in having to make such an enormous decision.

"Rachel, I'm sorry that this is hard for you. Please believe me, I do understand your dilemma but, if you really want me to open up this case, we have no other alternative…it's the only way I will be able to move forward to find out anything substantial for you and for everyone involved."

Finally and regretfully giving in she said, "If this really is the only way…if there is nothing else we can possibly do…well then…okay."

"Good. I'll go ahead and give the county examiner a call. I'll get any paperwork that has to be signed and notarized to you right away so that we can get things moving by the weekend."

"Thank you, Detective Danison. I'm sorry for being so difficult."

"Rachel, you're not being difficult. I do understand your misgivings about doing this. It's not at all easy, but I hope that you can understand where I'm coming from. I just want to be able to give you a quick answer and the best way to help us move on and get things done is by doing an exhumation."

"Thank you, Detective. I understand."

"Please call me Trevor, Rachel."

"Ooh…I guess that's only fair since I've asked you to do the same." Smiling, she said, "Okay, Trevor. I look forward to hearing back from you soon. Thanks again for taking the time to come by and look into this," she said as they stood.

"You're quite welcome," he said, putting his notepad into his jacket pocket.

"I'll show you to the door."

"Thank you."

Walking him to the door, Rachel began to feel a sense of relief in knowing that she could possibly get the answers she had been searching for, but after he left, she began to feel some remorse at having to break her promise to her Aunt Myra. *A cup of hot chamomile tea should help me to settle down,* she thought as she walked into the kitchen and put on a kettle of water. *I have to get my mind geared to the fact that there will be an autopsy. It has to be done no matter what.* Pensively, she sat at the kitchen table and determined that she would not to wallow in the decision—*there are other matters at hand that have to be taken care of. I refuse to take time out for a pity party*, she thought.

"Here you are. I was wondering where you disappeared to," said Anita as she entered the kitchen.

"Is everything alright? Is he working on the case?"

"Yes...he is," said Rachel sadly.

"Okay...what's wrong? I thought you'd be happy about this. Maybe you'll get some of those answers you're looking for. Why the gloom?

"I—um...I'm okay. It's just a little overwhelming...that's all. I'm happy about it. All is well."

Trying to skirt the issue and negating how she was really feeling, Rachel changed the conversation and said, "Anita, I need your help in clearing out Aunt Myra's closet and bedroom. I'm going to rearrange that room and use it as a guest room; I don't have enough strength to go through everything alone."

"Sure, Rachel. When you say everything, do you mean everything like the clothes, jewelry, shoes, and her books?"

"Oh...everything but not the jewelry and maybe we can leave the books. I'll take care of the jewelry and the books can stay on the shelves exactly as Aunt Myra left them. My mind has been so cluttered. I just don't have the energy to deal with all of the memories I'll find in there, let alone, just being in her room. Anita, when I open that door, I can still smell her scent...the lotion she used and how she smelled when we hugged or she kissed me on the cheek. I can't deal with it, Anita. Can you just hire someone to come in, organize everything, and give it away to a shelter or someplace? Maybe you can even call the church and see if we can donate everything to the Help Center. Aunt Myra was a very stylish lady, so the clothes can go just about anywhere."

Anita just stood there as she rambled on. No matter how much she tried to help her friend, she knew that there were no amount of words that would console Rachel to get through what she was now feeling. Removing those personal items would be like totally removing the memory of Aunt Myra from the house—this would be tough.

Tears began to well up in both their eyes.

"Okay, Rachel...let's not do this right now," said Anita wiping her own tears.

"I'll start getting some things together, but don't you think we should wait until after tomorrow's meeting? Ms. Myra may have already set up some provisions for everything in her will. That way, you're not stressing if things have already been taken care of."

"You know what? You're right! I really don't know what I'd do without you, Anita. Okay...we'll wait and see what happens before giving anything away. Call Attorney Wilkins to make sure everyone has been contacted?"

"Okay."

"Thanks, Anita." Rachel got up, added a bit of hot water and honey to her now warm tea cup and then walked into the sitting area with Anita. They talked and made plans for the meeting at the Dendell Conference House, unaware of danger lurking in the dark watching their every move through the open window shades of the French door of their home. Dressed in full black, an unidentified male is sitting in a dark colored Chevy Trailblazer, directly across the street in front of the park. He was monitoring their every move, using a high powered, professional, HD camera. Talking on his phone, he watched their every move. With the click of a camera and days of video footage, Rachel had become the subject of a personal docudrama and this mysterious man was the co-producer ever since the death of her Aunt Myra.

"Hey...yeah, this is Jess. She's in sight. Pretty little thing, she is. Yeah...okay. I'm enjoying this one. Don't worry. No hands will touch her until you give the go ahead. Yeah. That's been taken care of too...talk later."

Click...click...click went the camera as Rachel and Anita sat down on the sofa making plans for what was to come, unaware that there were even more dangerous plans being made for Rachel's future.

# CHAPTER 6
## The Intruder

A s Devin entered his apartment, he was hit hard from behind and shoved inside.

"Yeow!" He screamed as he hit the floor and a gun was immediately positioned on his temple.

Quietly, but demandingly, the intruder said, "Get up. Get up and don't you say one word."

Stunned, Devin got up staggering and blindly into his dark apartment.

"Who are you...what do you want?"

"I told you not to say a word!" Just sit down over there in that chair." Holding a bright flashlight in his gloved left hand, the attacker pointed to a chair next to the window in the living room.

"What do you want from me?"

"Arghh!" Devin yelled as he was punched in the stomach.

"Didn't I tell you not to say a word!!? I'll tell you when you can talk. Now shut up and sit down!"

Blinded by the light that now glared directly in his face, he stumbled back and fell into the chair. He couldn't see the face of his attacker who was dressed in black from head to toe because of the brightness that was directly in his face. It was then that Devin determined if he could not see his face, he would remember the voice. There was no way that this intruder who stood there before him, ordering him around and invading the privacy of his home would get away with this. In total desperation, Devin prayed as he sat there shaking, afraid of the unknown and what this person had planned for him. *Please, God…if I happen to live through this, help me to remember his voice…I've got to remember that voice…please God, please!*

The masked intruder took his foot and kicked the ottoman to the center of the room and sat in front of Devin. Reaching into his pocket, he took out a lighter and lit a cigar that he pulled from a stainless steel cigar and flask tube. Taking a few puffs, he blew into Devin's face, and said, "My people went to your aunt's house about three, maybe four weeks ago and didn't find that ruby ring and the other jewelry you were describing at the bar! I want to know where it is!! It was wasted time going there with no reward. So now, it's up to you to get it and bring it to me," he said laughing hauntingly. A serious look returned to his face and he said, "Know this, if you don't get it and bring it to me, that pretty little sister of yours is dead too!!"

"Dead too? What are you talking about? Who are you?"

"Oh. So now you don't remember. Hump! You were at Dizzie's Club talking to that singer named Delia. You caused quite a scene, I might add. Anyway, I was sitting right next to you and heard you talking about a ring that your sweet dear old Auntie had. You said it was worth thousands, so I had you followed. The next day, they went back and started looking around, but couldn't find anything where you said it would be. Your poor old Auntie caught my guys in the act of searching through her home and tried to get away. It's just too bad she had to fall down the stairs. Lucky for us, nobody touched her. She just fell all by herself...tumbling one step at a time, rolling down the stairs like tumbleweed blowing in the wind.

"Why you son of a—!" Devin jumped up and tried throwing a punch at his attacker, but missed and was quickly knocked back down into the chair. With one swift kick in the groin, the gun was now placed in his chest.

Devin fell back, crying out in excruciating pain, biting his lower lip and drawing a drop of blood.

"Ha! You stupid, drunken wimp. I can smell the liquor all over you. This place even reeks of its odor. You're going to get that ring for me and anything else of value or, like I said, your pretty little sister is going to die right along side you. She's being watched. Pretty cute broad. I could have a lot done to her just like I heard you did…eh?"

"How did you—"

"Just shut your mouth and listen. I'm going to be watching you and your sister. I'm not in this by myself. If you dare call the cops or talk to anyone else about this, you're a dead man and she'll be right along with you. Silent as if in contemplation, he added, "Hmm…your family can prepare a double funeral ceremony. Someone will die so watch your steps. You got it?"

Devin, still holding himself and praying that the pain would somehow relieve itself quickly said, "Yes…I got it! Got it!"

"I want that jewelry. You have 48 hours to get it. Wait on the logistics. Now I'm going to be a good little criminal and let you say what you need to say; wouldn't want you to hold anything back."

Before the intruder could get the last breath and word out, Devin shouted, "I don't even remember that conversation. I was probably drunk out of my head. I don't even know where that ring is."

Sarcastically, the intruder said, "Well, I guess you had better find out. Right?"

"Just where am I supposed to meet you if I find the ring and the jewelry?"

The intruder yelled, "Were you not listening? I just told you. Wait on the logistics. I'll let you know at the right time in the right place. Now, I'm thirsty. Get me an ice cold beer. I know you must have at least one in the fridge. I need something to quench my thirst, so it better be the coldest one you've got. Watch your step. Don't do anything you'll later regret."

With the pain in his groin substantially subsided, Devin walked away to get the beer as the intruder's phone rang.

"Yeah. I'm here with him. No! I told you...just watch her. Keep an eye on her, but don't touch."

When Devin returned, he was gone. Thankful to be alone now, he sat at the table with hands nervously shaking, pulled the tab on the can and chugged down the cold beer. In a state of fear with his mind running rampantly, Devin had a lot to think about with no time to waste in analyzing each piece of the puzzle that had just been laid out before him.

Like a crazy man, he was now talking out loud, having a conversation with himself saying, "Who was that guy? And how did this happen? I don't remember that conversation. He said I was with Delia at Dizzie's Club. I have to see her...she has to know what happened and what I said."

Devin jumped up, grabbed his jacket and keys and made a quick dash for the door. Delia was the only one who could help him understand and remember what he said and did that crazy night. He had to get to her quickly for answers to questions and without delay.

# CHAPTER 7
## Impetuous Talking

Rich vocal tones set the atmosphere as Delia Vandelyn performed on the stage at Dizzie's. There were regular patrons who came each night just to hear her jazzy renditions, and others came because they had heard about the woman with the velvet voice. Expressions of laughter and sometimes even tears, were exchanged in the intimate setting of the small club that sat on the corner of Brennan Boulevard and Stanley Way. Clapping, dancing and singing with Delia became a weekly ritual. Shouting accolades and applauding her at the end of her first set, they proclaimed,

"…Bravo…Bravo…"

"…More…More…"

"…Beautiful, Delia…"

"…Exquisite singing…"

"…Don't stop now…we want more…"

"… Sing, girl, you better sing that song…"

Overwhelmed by such love, Delia replied, "Thank you...Thank you so much. You're too kind, but I must take a short break and will be right back for the second set." As she exited the stage, the applause continued.

Walking over to the bar, one of her regular couples stopped Delia at their table and the gentleman said, "Delia...We really enjoyed you. Your voice is so beautiful."

"You made me cry tonight, Delia," said the woman.

Always humble, it was sometimes hard for Delia to accept personal compliments. Shyly she responded, "Thanks so much. I appreciate both of you very much."

"Will you sing the song 'Amazing Love' when you come back for the second set?"

"I sure will. Anything for my favorite newlywed couple."

"Can't wait!" said the woman with excitement. "Can we buy you a drink?"

"Why certainly. Thank you."

"Please tell Julius to put it on our tab. Get whatever you'd like... money is no issue."

"Okay, thanks so much, Mr. and Mrs. Chambers!" They smiled at each other and then kissed.

As Delia sat down at the bar, she sighed and said, "Julius...Please give me our very best red wine and credit it to the Chambers' tab. But first, can I have my hot tea with lemon, peppermint, and lots of honey. That was a hard set. I can't have the voice giving out on me now — I've gotten a few special requests," she smiled.

"Here you are, Delia...beautiful singing tonight."

"You're always on time with my tea — can't live without it. Thanks, Julius."

While Delia sat sipping on her tea concoction that always worked to soothe her tired voice, someone came up behind her and lightly covered her eyes. Tall, light brown hair and bluish-green eyes, he was dressed in a sky blue, open-collar shirt with navy blue dress slacks. Kissing her on the neck, he said, "Guess who?"

"Ooh...Well, let me see. The cologne smells mmm so good! And the voice sounds oh so familiar, smooth as silk like the honey in my tea...sounds like...Hmm...Garry!...Garry Briton?"

Excited, Delia jumped up, turned and hugged her friend as he planted a kiss on her cheek.

"Garry! Where have you been? I've missed you so much!"

While she spoke, he placed the tip of his finger on her ruby red lips and said, "Be quiet for a moment. I just want to look at you, gorgeous. I missed you too. I'm sorry for all the pain I caused you."

"But—"

"No, I want you to hear me. I know that you were only trying to help. I just got so overwhelmed. I thought you were like all of the other girls I've dated who were trying to get their hands into my pockets. My dad didn't help the situation any. He was putting a lot of negative ideas and energy into my head about you because you were not his ideal woman for me. I'm so sorry, Delia."

Pulling away from him, Delia said, "Hmm...So that's the reason. I had a feeling. Here, let's sit in my booth." She took him by the hand and led him to her reserved seating over in a secluded corner of the bar. When they sat down, she said, "I knew what was going on. From the first time I met your dad, I had this weird vibe about him. It was the way he looked at me. Then when he found out that I was a night club singer, that's when things really got ugly. I never told you this Garry, but he tried to get me to back away from you and the relationship by paying me off, offering me a lot of money to move away and make my home on the west coast. He said that if I did, he'd also hook me up with an agent when I got there. His one stipulation was that I could never, ever return and have no contact with you. He was so disgusting. He had me pinned up in a corner of the hallway and wouldn't let me move until I gave him an answer. It was only after Julius rescued me that he let me go.

"I know."

"You knew about it?"

"Only just recently. He told me about it right before he died. I don't think he really even meant to mention it. He was talking out of his head about something else and it slipped out. I think the drugs and morphine had a lot to do with it."

"Oh Garry. I'm so sorry! What happened? When did he die?"

"A month ago today. They found him in his office over a pile of paperwork passed out. They revived him and he survived a few days before he died...heart attack."

"Are you okay?" Delia asked, grabbing his hand.

"For the most part, yes. It's taking some time to get used to him not being here and running the company. But I'm good. I'm president now and I just needed to get things in order before seeing you."

Delia sat there seriously taking in all that Garry said and was beginning to get angry, and asked him, "Why are you here? It's obvious you believed everything that your father said about me."

"No—I didn't. I just didn't want to see you hurt. When I came to my senses and realized what he was trying to do, I confronted him and he threatened to expose you."

"Expose what?"

"Any and every little piece of dirt that he could find out or dig up about you was about to be exposed. The old man had hired an investigator. But I stopped him before he could get anything started. I love you too much and too deeply. I didn't want to see that happen and if there was anything to know, I didn't want to hear it or let him have the opportunity to dig dirt. So I had to back away and I apologize to you for that. Delia, you've never left my mind. I haven't been able to have an intimate relationship with anyone since then. I've kept myself busy with the company so that there would be no time for anyone else. I knew that one day we'd be back together again. You've always been the only one for me; that will never change."

Calming down a bit, she said, "Well, there wasn't really anything to be found out. I have a pretty good profile all over the Internet and social media. He wouldn't have hurt me in any way." Pausing to grasp in her mind what Garry had just said, she finally smiled and said, "It does make me feel better knowing that you were trying to protect me." Tilting her head to one side and looking into his eyes, she said, "I love you, Garry."

He got up from his seat, bent over and kissed Delia passionately.

Julius came over and said, "Uh… Excuse me, Delia."

Parting their lips, she said, "I know, Julius...time for my second set. I'll get my wine later."

"Yes, ma'am," he said, walking away.

"Garry, please don't go anywhere."

"I won't, my love. I will be right here, once again enjoying the time as I watch you on stage. I'll love every moment of it," he said, as he escorted her and the applause began again.

As she stepped up onto the stage, Devin rushed in. Seeing that it was too late to catch her before the set, he sat at the bar and watched.

*Wait...is that Garry Briton? What is he doing here? Scumbag,* he thought as he ordered a drink from Julius.

# CHAPTER 8

## Devin's Reality Check

Waiting for Delia to finish her set, Devin sat nervously encircling the top of his glass of vodka with his finger.

"Can I have a dish of lemon with salt?" Devin asked Julius.

"Sure."

Sitting the dish before him, Devin dipped the lemon in salt and began indulging in his unusual habit of sucking the salty wedges.

When the last note was sung, Delia said, "Good night, everyone and thanks for coming." She exited the stage. The applause seemed never-ending and was almost deafening to Devin. He stood and then thought that when Delia saw him, she would most certainly make her way over to him. But she didn't. She rushed back over to Garry and stood there talking and laughing.

Devin took his drink, walked up to the couple and sarcastically said, "Now what do we have here?"

Delia was surprised to see him and said, "What are *you* doing here? After the last time, Jason said that you were no longer allowed to step one foot in Dizzies?"

"What are you talking about? And since when did you hook back up with Mr. 'Drop Her like She's Hot' Briton?"

"Come on, man. It wasn't like that," protested Garry.

Delia jumped right in and said, "Anyway, it's none of your concern, Devin. What Garry and I do is between the two of us, so leave it alone—it's none of your business."

"Yeah…yeah. Whatever," he said, glaring at Garry.

Shifting his attention from Garry, he said to Delia, "You and I need to talk about the last time I was here."

"You're right; we do. You better be glad that Jason is out of town."

"Who…is…Jason?" Devin said in confused frustration.

"He's the owner of this establishment. Garry, do you mind waiting for me. I need to talk to my unbearable cousin for a minute."

"Sure, babe. I'll wait."

Devin grunted as he walked over to the bar. Delia followed behind him.

Sitting down, Delia said, "Julius, can I have that glass of wine now?"

"Sure, Delia…coming right up."

"Now Devin, the last time you were here, you were drunker than a smelly skunk. Jason said you were no longer allowed to sit in his bar."

Overhearing her, Julius said, "Is that right? I just served him vodka on the rocks!"

"Don't worry, Julius. I won't say anything, but just remember the next time."

"Thanks, Delia." Walking away, he mumbled, "Why doesn't anyone let me know anything around here?"

"I guess he takes his little job seriously," said Devin with a smirk.

"It's no little job and yes, he does. You can believe that this will be the last time you get a drink from him."

"Hmpf," Devin said, as he took a sip of his drink.

"Okay, so what happened the last time I was here at Dizzie's?"

"Oh. So you really don't remember?"

"No...don't remember a thing. Refresh my memory, Delia."

"First of all, you had a little buzz on when you walked through those doors. You started drinking more as soon as you sat down. Devin, you even ordered a few drinks for a couple of skank girls that were in here that night. I had finished my first set and was sitting at my booth, sipping my tea when you yelled over to me like a crazy man, all angry and what not. I had to calm you down. You were ranting and raving about how you couldn't stand Aunt Myra."

Devin shook his head when he heard that.

"Delia, exactly what did I say?"

Before responding, she took a sip of her wine and then said, "You couldn't believe that she took the keys to the house away from you, talking about 'what does she think— I'm going to steal the jewelry she has hidden up in her locked bedroom?' Then you started naming off all she had. You even tried putting everything in alphabetical order. You were louder than the crowd that was in here. People were laughing at you. It was so embarrassing for me. You were talking about my aunt, Devin—our aunt—like she was some mean old hag. I had to act as if we weren't related." Delia shook her head in disgust.

"Needless to say, my second set wasn't that great after having to deal with you and your outburst. Some of our regular patrons got up and left. Jason placed a hostess at the door to give out free meal and drink gift cards to entice them to come back another day. I couldn't believe how aggressive you had become when they tried putting you out of here. I convinced Jason not to call the police. You fell to the floor when security tried to drag you out of here. Yelling for them to leave you alone, you got up and staggered out on your own. I don't even know how you made it home as drunk as you were. I swore that I was not going to worry about you. I was so angry. I could have lost my job behind that, Devin."

Delia picked up her wine glass and sipped. She sat the crystal, long stemmed glass down and said, "How could you say those awful things about her after all she did for you? How could you, Devin?"

He couldn't believe himself either. Not wanting to go any further in the conversation or wanting to hear anymore, he stood and on his way out he mumbled, "Good night."

# CHAPTER 9

## George's Memory

George Vandelyn, the only brother of Myra Vandelyn, sat in the car waiting for his grand niece Delia to return from an errand she had to run on their way to the reading of the will.

Life was a struggle due to the fact that he was born mentally challenged. Myra's love for George helped him get through the many difficulties that plagued him. At times, the way he was treated hindered George as he worked hard to live a normal productive life. No matter what, Myra pushed him hard always telling him he could do anything that anyone else could do, and better. That encouragement helped George to make many successful strides in life. He greatly missed his big sister and was trying to shake the sadness he felt so deeply in his heart. Now, his main goal would be to remember everything she taught him so that he could make it on his own.

While waiting for Delia, he began thinking back to the last time that he visited Myra in her home and the conversation they had while sitting at the dining room table, coloring by number. This was one of his favorite pastimes and she always accommodated him by having the crayons and plenty of coloring books stashed away in the dining room cabinet.

*Picking up a red crayon and coloring the petals of a rose, George said to her, "Myra, do you know I love you? You are my 'bestest' sister in the whole wide world."*

*"And George, you are my 'bestest' brother in the whole wide world. I don't know what I'd do without you," she said, as she picked up a blue crayon to color in the sky above her picture of a team of Arabian horses.*

*"Myra, you are the only one who has ever understood me and took the time to listen and help whenever I needed you. Even when people thought I was just a dumb, old, stupid person, you took the time to help me get through it even with my learning disabilities."*

*"George, I told you that I never want to hear you say that... never again. You don't have a learning disability. You're smarter than anyone I know. As for me being the only one, I'm your sister... I'm supposed to love on you and help you. Look at you now, baby brother," she said, reaching over and hugging him tightly.*

"Well, you helped me to understand and get the education I needed. You will never, ever know how much that has blessed me. I love you, Myra."

"I love you too, George. You are my one and only brother and that's what sisters are for. Now how's that job coming at school?"

With a huge smile on his face, George couldn't contain himself and proudly said, "You know what? Yesterday they promoted me as head cook and I've got three people under me. They're good workers and we've been getting all kinds of awards and accolades for our tasty dishes."

"Oh, George, why didn't you tell me? I'm so proud and happy for you! You deserve it. You've really worked hard to get through that culinary school. Graduation is just around the corner and we're going to have to make an appointment with career counseling services to make sure they can help place you in a restaurant for your internship. Okay?"

"Okay, Myra."

"Now hand me a brown crayon for my horses," she said. For a moment there was silence as they concentrated on their artwork and then Myra said, "George..."

"Yes, Myra?"

"I can hardly wait to get another one of your coconut cream cakes."

"Really?" George said as he handed her the crayon.

"Yes...that is one of the best and moistest cakes I've had. The butter cream frosting with just a hint of lemon is *better than any store bought brand I've ever tasted. I haven't found one to match yours yet."*

*"Sis, if you have the ingredients we can go into the kitchen and I'll make you one right now."*

*"Really, George?"*

*"Uh-huh."*

*"Well I don't have anything here. But I'll tell you what...Let's go over to the market right now and get everything that you need to make that cake."*

*"Thank you, Myra," he said as he dropped the crayon onto the table now anxious to get to the market.*

*"No…thank you, George."*

Delia opened the car door, startling George out of his daydream. Tears began streaming down his face.

"Okay, Unkie George. The Dendell is right up the road. We'll get there in less than five minutes."

# CHAPTER 10
## The Will

Attorney Jovan Wilkins was all set and ready to execute the document signed by Ms. Myra Vandelyn. Everyone who was invited had graciously accepted the invitation to attend.

Since this would be a very emotional time for the family, he wanted to arrange everything to make things as light and manageable as possible. He began with creating an atmosphere of peace by playing a CD of music produced by Antoine "Beatz" Surgick. The music was very soothing, which helped to bring an air of calmness to the room.

Anita came early and began putting out boxes of Kleenex, pitchers of water, a coffee and tea brewer and, as directed by Aunt Myra, a tray of cinnamon sugar cookies—her favorite treat. Nightly, she would sit up in bed, sipping on a cup of hot lemon tea, eating the delicious delight.

The Dendell Conference House was the setting for this all important meeting. The room in which they would meet was beautiful and spacious. It was graced with two beautiful Schonbek DaVinci Crystal Pendant lights that were centered at each end of the room, surrounded by superb architectural crown molding.

The natural cherry wood casing that outlined each door and window was carved with exquisite floral designs that any artist or sculptor would, at first sight, fall in love with. A crystal sconce decked each side of the three entry ways, enhancing the beautifully carved wood.

Brazilian cherry wood flooring flowed throughout each room of this conference site. Burgundy accent chairs with gold design were positioned around a long rectangular table, making each guest feel important and well rested as they sat down comfortably within its cushioned base.

Slowly, they began to arrive. One by one—some two by two—were greeted by Attorney Wilkins and Anita and then taken to the refreshment table before being seated.

Rachel entered, followed by Pastor Freeman and Mother Hattie Larkin. As George and Delia entered, you could see that George was still in tears. He was really taking this hard.

After the death of Myra, Delia became quite concerned about her Uncle George, whom she affectionately calls Unkie. She promised herself to take up the mantle that was left void by her aunt and would be diligent in contacting him daily. Making sure that he'd continue to thrive in a way that would make Aunt Myra proud would most likely help George to also feel good inside.

Personal friends of Myra that were invited included Evelyn May who was just like a sister to her. The two of them had been friends for over eleven years. They had their arguments, but would always immediately reconcile their differences within the next hour. From the beginning of their friendship, they had vowed to never let anything get in the way of their sisterly relationship.

David Ducannon was also invited. There were suspicions that Myra and David at one point secretly married, but it had never been confirmed. After a failed marriage and the death of her second husband, Myra found it hard to make a commitment to marry again. That didn't stop the rumors of marriage from circulating, especially at church. It was a never ending cycle among the gossip mongers.

Addressed as Uncle David by family members, he was considered to be a genuine part of the Vandelyn family.

The only person who had not yet appeared was Devin. This was nothing unusual. His habitual lateness was known by all and had become generally expected. Devin would either be late or not show up at all. The irony was that you could always count on him to be on time and show up when it was for his benefit; he was selfish. Devin always put himself first before the needs of others.

It was about time to get started. Jovan walked over to Rachel and kissed her on the cheek saying, "Rachel, how've you been?"

"Oh, I'm good, Jovan," she said hugging him.

"I just want to get all of this over and done with. I really wanted to stay home and sleep. I think the stress of it all has finally worn me down and I've been having a hard time getting a good night's rest."

"It'll be over soon. We'll just wait a few more minutes to make sure that everyone's in place."

"Okay. That's fine with me. I'd like to visit with some of my family anyway. Oh, and if Devin isn't here soon, let's not wait on him. We'll just go ahead and get started."

"Are you sure about that?"

"Positively sure."

True to form, Devin never showed up. He had other plans in mind. Using duplicate keys to get in, he would have access to an empty house. Assured that his aunt would not think to leave him a thing in her will, especially after the way he treated her and had stolen from her, kept him away from the Dendell Conference House. Although he was forced to do it, this would be the perfect scenario in putting his plan into action to get his aunt's jewelry.

With the keys in the lock, he walked into the dimly lit house. Using a flashlight, he quickly scanned the room and uttered, "Good, they're gone. I need to find out where that jewelry is. It has to be somewhere in Aunt Myra's old bedroom." Running up the stairs, he stood in front of her door as he thought, *Hmm...and after all these years it's the one place I have never stepped foot in. It was her private sanctuary and no one was ever allowed in here.*

He turned the knob and muttered, "Dang! The door is locked." Pulling his wallet from his back pocket, he took out an old credit card and said, "Okay, now let me see if this trick will work to unlock this baby."

Sliding the credit card into the lock, he jiggled it around and moved it back and forth, trying several times without success. Almost giving in to defeat, he tried one last time after pulling the card out and sliding it in one more time, he exclaimed with joy, "Ah! It does work!"

He rushed in, stopped and first looked around admiring things he had never seen and then got down to the business at hand. "Now where would she keep it?"

The first obvious place he went to was her dresser. Bottles of cologne and perfumed scents were meticulously placed but, oddly enough, there was no jewelry in sight. From there, he began looking through drawers and the armoire. He worked carefully as not to break or get anything out of its original place. "Not in here. Maybe it's here?" "No," he angrily muttered as he looked from place to place. Devin was now starting to run around like a mad man looking under the bed, through the book-shelves, and any other place he thought it might be. His heart was racing and he tried calming himself so that he could think. As he sat down on the bed, he thought about the different places where he had already looked and where it might possibly be. *Now where else can it be if it's not here?* I know...the bathroom...under the sink?" Running in, he turned on the light and began perusing, moving things around, but this time he was not careful and wasted a box of laundry detergent onto the floor. Panic grew deep inside as he was not finding the jewelry box or anything that even looked like it could hold a piece of jewelry. In defeat he said, "It's not here. Where is it? I bet Rachel must have hidden it somewhere. I'll check her room. That has to be where it is," he said as he jumped up, made sure everything was in place, shut off the light, turned the lock on the doorknob and shut the door.

Yes, he left everything in its place, but failed to clean up the wasted detergent which caused him to leave his footprints on the moss green, deep shag carpet.

***

"Everyone, may I please have your attention. Thank you for coming out this evening for the reading of Ms. Myra Vandelyn's will. My name is Attorney Jovan

Wilkins. If everyone would please take your seat, we'll begin."

Perplexed, Uncle George asked, "Can we sit anywhere we want to?"

Rachel lovingly took Uncle George by the hand and said, "Yes, Uncle George. You can sit anywhere you would like. Why don't you come and sit right here next to me?"

"Okay. I'd like that very much, Rachel."

Anxious to ensure that the meeting would go well, Jovan said, "Alright then. Let's get started."

"Excuse me, Attorney Wilkins."

"Yes, Rachel."

"If you don't mind, I would like for Pastor Freeman to offer a word of prayer before we proceed."

"No. I wouldn't mind that at all."

"Thank you. Pastor Freeman, the floor is yours," said Rachel nodding her head to him.

"Please bow your heads and close your eyes in reverence to God. Thank you," he said with a smile as he began to pray, "Father in heaven, we ask Your divine blessings over these Your people as we go forth in the reading of this will. Please let Your hand of mercy, grace and favor be upon each one sitting here in Your presence. Let it guide and protect us. Give all Your perfect peace and let Your divine will be done. In Jesus' name we pray. Amen." Everyone responded with, "Amen."

"Thank you, Pastor Freeman. Now, let us begin," said Attorney Wilkins.

"I'm going to keep this as brief and simple as possible for everyone and just go according to how it's been written. This document is dated June 10, 2008 and the letter attached was hand written by Ms. Myra Vandelyn. It is also notarized on the same date by yours truly.

*To my family members and friends,*

*If you are reading this will, it means that I have gone on to be with my Father God in heaven. I am only hoping and praying that my life was one that was exemplary and could be emulated by others.*

*To keep things in line and order driven, I have asked my attorney to write checks for each of you and place them in separate envelopes. As all of you know, I have never liked any kind of formality. Therefore, I don't want this event to be one of formality. I have prayed about this and God has helped me to treat each one of you according to what we feel you deserve. There is no need for Attorney Wilkins to call off each amount you have received. What you have been given is what you well deserve. I pray that it will be a blessing and that you will use the money in a way that will help you to not only bless others, but will help you succeed in the rest of your life. As God told Adam: "Be fruitful and multiply," so that you will be prosperous in all that you do. I love you all very deeply.*

*Now let's get started. First, I'd like to address the person that is so very important to me. Please...I'm begging you to please help George to continue with his professional chef education at the Elite School of Cuisine. Support him in every way and love on him. He is a quiet, gentle spirit and will need your guidance. I am sure that I can count on you, Delia and Rachel, to make sure that this occurs. George, I love you so much. Please don't give up. Please stay strong and make me proud of you. I'm watching you from heaven and will always be your special guardian angel. So never give up and don't be afraid to do all that you can. Work hard to achieve your goals. Remember everything that you've learned and have been taught.*

Hearing these words was a bit too much for George and he began to weep. Both Rachel and Delia embraced him, trying to give him comfort.

"Mr. Vandelyn, are you okay?" Attorney Wilkins asked with genuine concern as he laid the papers down.

Trying to catch his breath, and not hyperventilate, George said, "Yes. I'm fine." He then wiped away his tears and blew his nose.

"Okay then, let's continue with the reading," said Attorney Wilkins, picking up the paper.

*Rachel, stay strong and be the woman of worth that you already are. Stay true to yourself and don't let life get you down. Have fun, baby girl. Stop taking life so seriously. In addition to your check, I want you to have all of my jewelry and the house. Keep the jewelry in a safe place — especially away from Devin. No telling what that thief will do if he finds it. I love you.*

Tears trickled down Rachel's face, blurring her vision. George, patted her on the back and whispered, "It's okay to cry Rachel...its okay."

*To my sweet Delia, you are a gift from God. Music is your ministry because it soothes the soul, mind and heart. Continue singing and sharing the gift that God has blessed you with. My sincerest prayer is that you take this gift back to the church where you know it belongs. Don't give up what you're doing, but don't forget about the one who gave you the amazing gift of song. Please pray about it. I know that you will be welcomed with open arms.*

Delia looked up toward the ceiling, not wanting to see any expression that may have now appeared on the face of Pastor Freeman. This was not the first time the topic had been discussed. A lone tear dropped from her chin to the table.

*To David, my precious love — thank you for the times we shared with each other. My love for you will always remain even in death. And to all inquiring minds, David and I had never married — we were just very close friends, who took many trips together because we needed each other for friendship and traveling companionship. We saw a lot of places and shared the many sights of this world, but always had separate rooms in every beautiful hotel we were fortunate to stay in. David, continue to be all that God requires of you. You are truly a great man of wisdom and strength. Don't stop living and having fun. Do all you can to be all that you can especially for the kingdom of God. Missions are calling you!*

David smiled with glistening eyes as he listened to the words she had written for him alone.

*To my sister friend, Evelyn, I thank God for you and the many years of fun we shared being mischievous and getting away with it. I hope your amount helps to open that little bistro on the beach we've talked so much about in Anguilla. I know that your heart is in giving to others, but don't give away too much! God wants you to also be fulfilled and have the riches of this world. Make it a reality, my friend. Much love, stay sweet.*

"I will, Myra...I promise you, I will," she softly said.

*Anita, thank you for all the help you've given as an assistant in our household. You truly have a servant's heart. God is going to bless you beyond measure because of that attribute. It is now up to you as to whether or not you would like to continue on with Rachel. I leave that decision to you. Whatever you decide, please know that you will be very blessed not just in the present, but in the future.*

Turning away, Anita hid her face as the tears flowed down her cheeks.

> *Pastor Freeman, I am hoping that Rachel invited you to this celebration. You are a hard-working man in God's kingdom. The rich word you serve to God's people can never be compared to any other. You are a blessing to the body of Christ. Attorney Wilkins has a special gift to the church to be used for the children's missionary fund. Maybe you can get that new room decorated for them. Thanks so much for your ministry gift. May God continue to bless you!*

Pastor Freeman looked over at Mother Hattie Larkin, who was crying and nodded his head, saying softly, "Praise be to God."

> *Devin, I bequeath to you not one single copper penny and that's all that needs to be said. You probably didn't show up anyway. So there is no more to be said neither to you nor about you. You're just who you are. Even with all the bad in you, I never stopped loving you, but never wanted to deal with the agony of your defeated life. Devin, it's time for you to stop and think about how you are living. Embrace life in a righteous manner and blessings will someday become yours.*
>
> *Sincerely,*
> *Myra Vandelyn*

There was not a dry eye in the room as they sat there trying to comprehend all of the wisdom she had just shared with each one of them. This was not just about money, but it was about living a fruitful life. Tissue boxes were being passed from one end of the table to the next.

Even Attorney Wilkins seemed to have been affected by what he had read, and he sat there for a moment trying to let things settle before continuing. He then said, "Thus ends the reading of the will as bequeathed from Ms. Myra Vandelyn. As stated in the reading, an envelope for each of you has been set aside, with a very sizable check endorsed in each of your names and a copy of what I have just read. If you have any questions, please feel free to ask me and I will be glad to address any concerns you may have at the end of this meeting. Thank you for coming."

"Pastor Freeman..."

"Yes, Rachel."

"Please know that I will also be making a sizable donation to the church on Sunday morning."

"Well, thank you very much. It will go a long way in taking care of some much needed repairs."

"Pastor, if you don't mind, I'd like to have one of the rooms dedicated in the name of my aunt. Is that possible?"

"Sure. No problem. Just come by the office and we can decide which room you'd like."

"Thank you, Pastor Freeman, but I think it's appropriate to say that the children's ministry is the perfect room to name after Aunt Myra. They meant a lot to her."

He shook his head in agreement and as they talked, Devin walked in.

"Well look who decided to show up after everything is over," said Rachel sarcastically.

"Yeah, I'm here. What did I get? What did she leave for me, Rachel?"

"Honestly, Devin. Did you think she would leave you a thing? Did you really?"

"Well, it doesn't hurt to ask, does it, Rachel," he spat.

"See Jovan to get a copy of what Aunt Myra left you — words of wisdom."

"I don't need any words from a dead corpse."

"Dear God, please forgive him and touch his heart in Jesus' name," said Pastor Freeman as he and Mother Larkin walked away.

Everyone else stopped in shock and horror at hearing what he said. They looked at Devin with disgust and made him feel very uncomfortable, so he turned to leave. Walking away, he stopped and asked, "Where's the jewelry? Who got the jewelry?"

"That's really none of your business — is it, Devin?" Delia said in a stern but controlled voice as she took George by the arm and walked away from the room.

"Come on, Uncle George. Let's go before he contaminates us with his selfishness."

"Okay, Delia, let's go. Goodbye, everyone."

"Goodbye, George."

Devin was now frustrated. Even though he knew there was a possibility that he would be left out of the will, it still troubled him not to have information about the jewelry. He was desperate to get it since he had looked all over the house and could not find it anywhere. He desperately needed answers. Time was running out. What would he do now? He had to find the jewelry or be killed — possibly with Rachel at his side. Lives were now hanging in the balance.

# CHAPTER 11

## No News is Good News

D ing dong.

"Anita, someone's at the door. Anita! Hmm...where in the world is she? Anita!"

"I'm here. Sorry about that. My stomach is a little bit queasy. I think I ate too much of the wrong thing last night. I'll get it."

"It may be Detective Danison. He might have some news for me today. If it is, send him right in," said Rachel as she shut down her laptop and placed it in the bottom drawer of her oval shaped mahogany desk.

Anita hurried to answer the door as it rang again.

Waiting for her guest, Rachel thought, *Aunt Myra, you are something else. That letter you wrote was a real blessing and I'm going to do what you said. I first have to make sure that your death was just a mere accident.*

"Hello, Rachel." As she looked up, Trevor stood there with a big smile on his face. Rachel could not help but smile back and thought *he's so cute with his beautiful, white teeth* and then said, "Detective Danison, thanks for returning. I got your message about coming here today," she stood and walked over to him.

"I've been so distraught over losing my aunt and I hope you have some news that will free me from the enormity of these feelings that I've been holding on to regarding her death."

"Rachel, first remember that you agreed to call me Trevor."

"Oh, that's right. I'm sorry, Trevor. My mind's just been devoid of so many things lately. Please excuse my forgetfulness."

"No need for apologies. There's just no reason for us to be so formal with each other. I like it better that way, if I must say so myself," he said with an even bigger smile.

"I do too. But please, can we just get down to the business at hand?" Rachel said trying not to blush.

"Sure…excuse the digressing."

"Did the coroner find anything when Aunt Myra's body was exhumed?"

"Sorry, Rachel…he didn't. There's no conclusive evidence to show that something out of the ordinary caused her untimely death. She must have slipped and fell down the stairs. Here's a copy of the report. If she was pushed, we have no way of proving that either. I'm not sure if this is what you wanted to hear or not, but it's all we have. Tell me, why do you doubt what happened? Is there something you're keeping to yourself and not telling me?"

"I—I don't know. I just have this achy, gnawing feeling. I've had it since the day I got that call saying she was in the hospital. I can't believe I was wrong. I guess I just need to try and erase it all from my mind and get on with life. My aunt said that I should have fun, be myself and stop taking life so seriously. I've always been one to think too much and too deeply. I've been told that I'm too analytical for my own good. I guess that's what I've been doing this time too."

Feeling defeated, she said, "Well, it's time to let it go and let Aunt Myra rest in peace."

"Rachel, I'm not trying to push or be presumptuous, but I know you've been through a lot lately. I'd really like to take you out to dinner. Besides, you wouldn't want to let your Aunt Myra down. Would you? It'll help take your mind off of those deep things and thinking too much."

As he spoke, Rachel couldn't help but notice his perfectly shaped lips and thought, *He does have everything I want and need in a man.* Trying to send that thought away from her mind and not wanting to seem anxious about him and his dinner proposal, she coyly said, "Now hold on Trevor. I wasn't saying this to get a date out of you."

Anita walked into the room, interrupting and said, "I'm sorry, but I couldn't help overhearing Detective Danison's dinner invitation and I think it's a great idea,

Rachel. You should go and enjoy yourself for a change. Get out of the house...you know?"

With a slight tone of aggravation, Rachel replied, "Anita, no one was asking your opinion."

Unhindered, she said, "Well, I'm just saying...you need this. You've been too stressed and you need to get up and out of the funk."

Trevor laughed and Rachel bashfully released a smile and said, "Okay...okay, but just let me think about it. Trevor, I'll give you a call later on today."

"Sounds good. Here. These are my personal telephone numbers." He gently placed a card in her hand and said, "If I hear anything else regarding your aunt, I'll let you know, Rachel, but I really want to hear from you.

Forcing a smile, she said, "Thanks for all of your help, Trevor."

"I'll see you out, Detective," said Anita.

"Thanks, Anita," he said with eyes still focused on Rachel.

"Anita...Can I see you after you're finished?"

Not unnerved by Rachel's demeanor, she replied, "Okay."

As they walked out the door, Rachel stood there with a disappointed heart. There was no closure in her quest to get answers. Against her better judgment, she decided to leave it alone. She would no longer pursue the questions that she allowed to take over her mind and her life. It was time to move on.

Looking from the window, she watched Trevor drive away and thought, *I guess I was wrong about everything. I need to get myself together and not be so serious like Aunt Myra said. Hmm…Trevor is handsome with his gray-blue eyes and edgy haircut. He dresses and smells nice too. I think I could get used to him. He seems friendly enough, but I don't really know anything about him to date him. I'll have to call Jovan and ask a few questions before I make that step. You know, I'll bet this was a set up for a blind date from the very beginning. He's always trying to pull something over on me. Hmm…I'm trapped. I'm really trapped.*

"Rachel…"

She turned around with arms folded and said, "Well, Anita. Aren't you the one."

"Huh…what do you mean, Rachel?"

"Stop playing games…You know what I'm talking about. You shifted me into an awkward position with Trevor."

With a smirk, Anita replied, "Oh, it's Trevor now and not Detective Danison."

"We both came to a mutual understanding that we didn't want to be so formal with each other. He's kind enough to take care of this matter, free of charge, on his off hours."

"Hmm…I do think it would be nice for you to go out with that handsome gentleman."

"I guess. But I need to speak with Jovan first. I've got some questions for him. I don't know Trevor and who he really is. I just need some answers before I move any further with this."

"Really...okay. I'll put that call into Jovan and see what I can find out. Hey, did Detective Danison have any news about the case for you?"

"No. He said the coroner's report shows no foul play...it's inconclusive."

"Well, that's a good thing. You can stop worrying about it now. It's sad that we had to lose Aunt Myra in this way, but there is nothing that can be done to bring her back. It's time to move on and enjoy life to the fullest. That's what she wants us to do and we need to get on with it."

"You're right. It's just hard being in this big old house without her." Rachel stepped away from the window, sat at the desk and picked up a picture of Aunt Myra and herself, lovingly staring at it.

"I know it's going to be hard. It'll take some time, but you'll get used to it. She wants you to be happy, Rachel. I'll call Jovan for you," she said walking away.

"Thanks, Anita. Oh, and will you make arrangements to put Auntie's jewelry in a safe deposit box at the bank? I don't feel comfortable wearing it right now. I want to wait until things settle in my mind."

Standing at the door entryway, she proudly said, "Oh, that's already been taken care of. We took it yesterday after the reading of the will. Jovan made all the arrangements. Now Devin won't be able to get his hands on any of it. Mr. Wallace, the bank manager, said they'll do an appraisal and get the information back to Jovan. He'll let you know as soon as it's prepared."

"Thanks for being proactive, Anita."

"You're welcome, Rachel. Oh, and all of the clothing and shoes are all packed and ready to go. Pastor Freeman is having Deacon Charles and Walters come by with the truck later on today to pick up the boxes. I just have a few minute details to take care of and I'll be finished getting some other things together."

Rachel sighed, feeling a lump in her throat that would try to bring up the tears she felt forming in her eyes. This was it. The last signs of life... once they were removed from the house, she would ultimately have to move on.

Ignoring what she could see happening, Anita continued giving details. "I also called Revitalizing Klean to come in and give the room a thorough cleaning. They'll get it totally cleaned and smelling fresh. You'll be able to walk in there and smell nothing but pine fresh...just as clean smelling as the great outdoors," Anita said thinking she could get a smile from Rachel. It didn't work so she walked away. Anita then knew that this was another time of mourning and no amount of joking would help Rachel get beyond the sadness. Rachel needed to be alone.

# CHAPTER 12
## Down to the Wire

Through the bay window of his multi-million dollar home, Michael Stern stood watching and waiting for Jess, an employee in his organization. Jess was the one who did all of his dirty work, but there were times when Michael took care of things himself, as in the case of Devin Vandelyn. It wasn't about the jewelry; it was about what Devin did to his sister, Melinda. Because of this, Michael wanted to make a bold statement and give Devin a part of his undying misery.

Devin Vandelyn was on his hit list. He had to take care of this business and teach him a major lesson he would not soon forget. Devin was the cause of his sister's death.

Michael had never met Devin due to living in another state at the time. They had only talked once on the phone when Melinda called Michael to make the announcement to her big brother. It was a wedding that, unfortunately never happened.

Michael was present on the wedding day, sitting in the very last pew, waiting to escort his sister down the aisle of the Saint Mary's Episcopal Church. Suddenly, he heard a scream echoing throughout the sanctuary that shattered the silence. Melinda was told that Devin was not there and would not be attending. Hurt by this devastating news, his sister fell to the floor and was rushed to the local hospital.

Devin had left her at the altar. With a sanctuary of over six hundred guests, she had to tell them that the wedding was off. All the plans Melinda had made to marry him were flushed down the toilet, leaving her embarrassed and in debt...Michael's debt. Family and friends enjoyed a reception that was missing a happy, newly married couple. It devastated Michael to see the state that this rejection left his baby sister in. No one was allowed to hurt her and get away with it. Devin had a price to pay and Michael would see to it that it was paid in full.

Jess finally made it to the mansion. Walking into the main living area, he asked, "Did he get it?"

"No...claims he has no idea where it is. He has a few more hours to get the jewels together."

"Are you really going to kill him and his sis?" Jess asked, rubbing his hands together.

"Hmm...maybe...maybe not. But he'll be in the hot seat wondering which way things will go. He just better have what I want before the day is out. In the meantime,

find him and give him a little reminder to get it together...and quickly. Check his apartment first and be careful
not to kill him or be seen...I personally want that
job...This is for my sister."

"Wait...Is he the one that—"

"Yes...He's the one."

With a smirk on his face, Jess said, "Man, I didn't
think it was about the jewelry. You've got more than
your share. Boss, I'll give him a reminder that will be
hard to ever forget. Melinda was my girl and this guy has
got to pay for what he did to my little sis."

"Just don't kill him. I want him to know who I am
when the right time comes to deal with it."

"You still want me to watch his sister?"

"Ah...No...I guess not. Leave the pretty little thing
alone for right now. I think I want to get to know her
myself. She's cute."

"And I wanted her for myself," said Jess sarcastically.

"Hump...she's mine," said Michael as he sat on the
window bench, pulled a cigar from a case in his suit
pocket and lit it.

"Alright...I'll go take care of Devin."

"Check in with me once you do it. Then follow him.
Once you find out what he's doing, come back and take
Mildred with you."

Frowning, Jess asked, "Mildred, your housekeeper?"

"Yes...I'm going to have Mildred make the pickup.
I'm trying to keep things cool with Rachel and Mildred is

a nice lady—soft spoken, but trustworthy. She'll get the package and then you bring it here to me."

"You serious, Boss?" Jess asked with skepticism.

"Yes…I am."

"Okay. Whatever."

***

"Hello?"

"Hey, Rachel…it's Devin."

"And what do you want?" Rachel said agitated.

"Can't a brother call his sister without having his motives challenged?"

With a long sigh, she said, "Come on, Devin. Every time you call, you're either up to no good or you want something. So which is it? What is it that you want today?"

"Can I come over? I need to talk to you about something pretty important."

"Why can't we just discuss whatever this pretty important stuff is over the phone now?"

"I need to see you and it has to be done face to face. There's not much time. So can I come over now?"

"You sound suspect."

Angrily, he said, "Come on, Rachel. This is serious!"

"Okay…okay, but you have to make it quick. I have a dinner date."

"A dinner date? With who?"

"None of your business. So if you need to come here, then do it. But make it quick."

"I'm on my way."

He slammed the phone down and quickly grabbed his keys. Opening the door, he was once again pummeled and hit in the stomach as Jess said, "Surprise!"

Pain gripped Devin and he yelled, "arghhh!"

Falling to the floor, he was kicked in the ribs as his attacker said, "This is just a little reminder. You have three hours left to get the jewelry or else."

"Oughhhh....Oww!" Holding his stomach, Devin tried hard to suppress the intense agony he was feeling.

Painfully he said, "I'll get it...I will!"

"Tell your sister, Rachel, I said, Hi. It was nice watching her the other night."

Glaring at his attacker, he asked, "You...you were stalking my sister?"

"Yes. She's a cute chick. She needs to be careful when she leaves that mansion. She might just run into a little mishap...It's just not safe anywhere anymore. Now do what you have to do and fast!" He quickly exited the apartment. Devin was left sprawled in pain on the floor.

Trying to catch his breath and balance himself, he said, "I've got to get to Rachel!"

# CHAPTER 13
## Desperate Situation

"Rachel, Devin is here."

"Yes, I'm here," he said sarcastically as he pushed his way past Anita, still trying to mask his pain.

"Well, excuse me," she said, crossly looking at him.

"You're excused."

Shaking her head in disgust, she said, "Devin, you are so rude."

"You know you like it, Anita."

"*Arrrghhhh*! I just can't ...you are so irritating!" Anita said in anger.

"Calm down, Anita," said Rachel. "You just can't train this dog new tricks...Sometimes you just have to put up with the stink of his poop."

Devin stood there laughing, but still inconspicuously holding his side.

Glaring at him, Anita said, "And he smells mighty nasty." Turning her attention away from him, she said,

"Rachel, I'm going out to take care of some personal errands. Do you need anything while I'm gone?"

"No...I don't think so. Thanks. Take some time and relax while you're out. Go see Jovan..."

"What?"

"Come on, Anita. I know the two of you are dating. It's no secret...I see the way you two look at each other."

"I'm not admitting anything, but I'll take it under consideration, thank you..." she said with a smirk.

"You're welcome," said Rachel smiling.

Impatient, Devin said, "Come on you two, my time is running out... I've got business to take care of and you're messing with my schedule."

Shaking her head and taking a deep breath, Anita said, "I'll be back in about an hour or so, Rachel. Call if you need anything."

"Will do."

Closing the door behind her, Anita left Devin and Rachel alone. Rachel walked over and sat down on a white leather sofa adjacent to the built-in wall bookshelf, which was filled with books on every subject imaginable. Myra Vandelyn was an avid reader—a library of knowledge on every subject. Ask any question and Aunt Myra would answer it with great intelligence. She could stand up to a professor or educator at any level and could compete with an expert's mastery of knowledge.

Her favorite television show was Jeopardy. Friends and family encouraged her to audition for the show on several occasions. But being a very private person, she refused to flaunt her intellect in public. In this room, that held vast pages of knowledge, her nephew, Devin, who she tried to raise like a son would ask Rachel to do a hard thing. This matter of life and death would not go away very easily.

"Rachel...I need something from you," he said intensely.

"And ask me if I'm surprised, Devin," Rachel said, rolling her eyes up to the ceiling. She digressed within her mind and wondered if God would be okay with her tossing a book or two at her brother who clearly did not understand the strain she was under while she continued to mourn the passing of their aunt. Was he seriously asking her for something? Now? If Aunt Myra was here she probably wouldn't mind. But hitting your annoying, selfish brother with Aunt Myra's books wasn't the way to deal with Devin. Rachel prayed that God would give her strength to deal with him. This would not be easy — nothing with him was.

"Rach...come on. Give me a break. If I don't do this, some serious things will happen. I'm sorry; I really messed up bad this time. I need your help or both of us are in grave danger."

"Devin, what do you mean? What kind of danger?"

"Let me start from the beginning."

"Uh-oh...What is it now?"

"Well, a few weeks ago, I was at the Dizzie's Bar and Grill talking to Delia. She was performing there. She's pretty good and she—"

"Devin, just get to the point."

"Oh well...You know how I get. I was a little drunk and—"

"A little drunk, Devin?"

Irritated, he said, "Come on, Rachel, just let me finish."

Rachel began to think, *Oh no... what's next... God, please give me strength to deal with this. I just know it's going to be bad.*

"I was drunk and I was talking all out of my head. I didn't know what I was saying, Rachel. I was torn up and I guess I said some things a little too loud."

"What do you mean, a little too loud? What did you say, Devin?" Rachel's heart began to pound hard and fast.

"I was talking about Aunt Myra. I was upset about what happened between the two of us and her throwing me out of the house and treating me like some stranger and taking away my house keys. Some guy sitting there at the bar heard my ranting and raving."

Impatient for him to get to the point, she asked, "So what's that got to do with anything? What's the purpose of all of this? Get to the point, Devin."

"Well...I started talking about all she had and her jewelry and—"

Rachel stood up and got face to face with Devin. "Wait...You with your drunk, broke down, belligerent self let a complete stranger know about Aunt Myra and the jewelry in the house? What's next, Devin? I really don't want to hear it because I know it has to be something really bad."

Devin began pacing the floor nervously as he said, "Sis...that next day, they broke into the house."

"What? No, Devin...no!"

Rachel stood there in shock, trying to take in the enormity of what Devin had just revealed to her.

"Oh, my God! No! What have you done, Devin? The house was broken into...When? When was it, Devin? Wait! Oh no...dear God...Aunt Myra! Was it because of them? Were they the ones that...I knew it!! I knew it!! I have to call Detective Danison now!"

Pulling her back before she could reach the phone, Devin yelled, "No, Rachel! Don't call anyone. They've been watching both of us and you can't call anyone...You can't do it!"

"Watching me?" Rachel felt the horror of it all race through her body.

"Yes, Rachel...They've been stalking you and you can't call anyone. They're probably out there right now watching the house," he said, as he peeked out the window for anything strange.

Rachel felt light-headed and fell onto an adjacent lounge seat. She could not compose herself and began to cry uncontrollably. All she could think about was what her aunt must have gone through when she came face to face with the intruders. Looking at Devin, hatred swelled deeply in her heart. She tried for so long to get rid of this hatred by praying and seeking professional counseling. Devin had been an intruder in her life for much of her youth as he controlled life by sexually molesting her in the secret place of her bedroom night after night. Embarrassment and fear kept her quiet as she dealt with this dirty little secret that had caused her many sleepless nights.

It stopped at the age of sixteen when she had enough of his nasty abuse. Hiding a kitchen knife carefully beneath her bed covers, she stabbed him in the penis as he laid his hot, sweaty body upon hers one stormy and rain-drenched night. Bleeding profusely, Devin jumped from the bed, screaming in pain. Through tears, Rachel threatened to kill him if he ever touched her again.

That was the end of his escapades into her private space. He never touched her in that way again. He feared for his life and for some time was left with an embarrassing scar that led him to drinking as he fought off the demons of sexual immorality. For a while, he struggled because he thought that he would never be able to perform in the same way again. Several surgeries helped him to gain back what was lost, but his game of controlling Rachel was over. Now, here he stood, getting ready to beg her to do something he knows she'll have trouble agreeing with.

"What have you done, Devin? It's your fault that she's dead. You did it!! You helped to kill Aunt Myra!"

"You can't possibly blame this on me. I wasn't there!"

"But you caused it to happen. If you hadn't opened your foul drunken mouth, it wouldn't have happened. She would still be here. She'd still be here with me!"

Tears burned Rachel's eyes as she once again mourned the death of her Aunt Myra. Again she cried uncontrollably, unable to contain herself.

Taking her by the shoulders, Devin shook her and said, "Rachel...Rachel...Snap out of it. I need the jewelry. Where is it?"

Through angry tears, she said, "I'm not giving you her jewelry."

"She's no longer here. Did she give it to you? Is it yours now?"

Pulling away from him, through angry tears she said, "Yes, Devin...it's mine and you are not getting it!"

Devin pulled a pile of tissue from a box that sat on the desk and squatted down next to Rachel, and said, "Rachel, look at me...Wipe your eyes and look at me. I need for you to pay attention to what I'm saying so look at me. Here...take this tissue...Wipe your eyes and blow your nose."

Rachel snatched the tissue out of his hand and did as he said.

"Now listen to me, girl...I need that jewelry or they are going to kill both of us."

Rachel could not believe what she was hearing and jumped up from the lounge chair. "No...you're lying to me. You're making this story up just to get the jewelry. I refuse to believe you because I don't want to believe that Aunt Myra had to go through what she did with those intruders! I can't and I won't believe you!"

"Rachel...I'm not lying to you. If you have never ever believed me before, you have to believe me now. I was given 48 hours...I only have a few hours left before they'll be back."

Seeing the unbelief written all over her face, Devin began unbuttoning his shirt.

Backing away from him, she yelled, "What are you doing? If you try to put one finger on me, I swear I'll kill you!" She ran to the desk and tried to open the drawer for a gun that she kept hidden in a secret compartment of the desk.

"Rachel, cool it! I'm not going to touch you...I just want to show you something."

She stood there nervously leaning on the desk. As he opened his shirt, Rachel saw that Devin's stomach and chest were covered with contusions—red, black and blue welts all over his body.

"Rachel, look at me. This is the reminder I was given."

"Devin! What happened?"

"I was beaten, Rachel...I'm black and blue all over and in a lot of pain right now. Do you believe me now?"

Not really wanting to believe what was happening, but knowing that now she had to go along with what he was saying, Rachel gave into Devin. She now believed that he had actually gotten them involved in a dangerous situation and could be killed.

"Where's the jewelry, Rachel?"

"It's in a safe deposit box at the bank," she flatly stated, having become more resigned to the fact that she was now a major part of whatever negotiations Devin had incurred. In this moment of time, it was hard for Rachel not to hate her brother even more.

"Rachel, we have to get it...We have to go now!"

Grabbing her by the arm, Devin rushed Rachel out the door. They had a limited amount of time to make it to the bank before it closed.

# CHAPTER 14

Rachel Hands Over the Jewelry

Michael Stern sat at his desk thinking back to his conversation with Mildred, his housekeeper.

*Mr. Stern, is it okay for me to dust your office?*

*Mildred, let's put the dusting off for today. I have an errand that needs attention.*

*An errand?*

*Yes. Today you're going to take a little trip with Jess. I need for you to get a package for me. I'll let you know more once I hear back from him.*

The phone rang, interrupting his thoughts.

"Hello?"

"Yes, boss. This is Jess. We're here at the First Plymouth Bank. Devin's sister Rachel just went inside. I guess this must be where the jewelry is."

"Put your speaker on so that Mildred can hear."

"Okay, boss."

"Mildred..."

"Yes, Mr. Stern," she nervously said.

"This is the errand. You're looking for a lady named Rachel Vandelyn to come out of the bank. Jess will point her out to you. When she comes out, do not ask her any questions. Even though Jess has identified her, I want you to confirm that she is Rachel. You are not to answer any questions that she may ask. When she confirms who she is, tell her to hand over the box of jewelry that was left by her Aunt Myra and let her know that her brother, Devin, told your boss about it...nothing more...nothing less. It's a matter of life and death. Do you think you can handle it Mildred?"

Mildred was hesitant about doing it. But she knew if she didn't, there would be some kind of consequence to pay.

With tears welling in her eyes, she said, "Yes, I can sir, but this doesn't sound good...It makes me nervous. I don't want to get into any trouble for doing something that's outside of the law. I've had enough trouble in my life and have served my time. I enjoy life too much to lose it again by doing something that's wrong, sir."

"Are you crying? Okay, you must remember, Mildred, I'm the one who got those charges reversed and out of the system. Yes, you served a few months, but it was me who worked my tail off to get you released. So you owe me. I've got people in high places, so stop worrying about something that won't happen. There's no problem.

All you're doing is picking up the box. Once you have it, get back into the car and come straight here. Okay?"

Sniffing and wiping tears from her eyes, she softly said, "Yes, Mr. Stern."

Trying his best to soothe her worries, he said, "That's my Mildred. There will be an extra bonus in your check this week. Okay?"

"Yes, Mr. Stern. Thank you."

***

Devin waited in the car while Rachel made the transaction with the bank. Paranoid, his eyes roamed back and forth looking into his rear view and side mirrors — watching for any and every movement. He was afraid that at any moment he would be attacked once again. Impatience grew as he waited for Rachel to walk out of the bank with the boxed jewelry. Regret traced the corners of his mind as he thought about the person he was and who he had become over the years. His life was a messed up, miserable one and he knew it.

Finally, Rachel came out of the bank with the box. As she walked toward the car, she was suddenly approached by a woman, who asked "Are you Rachel Vandelyn?"

"Yes, I am. Can I help you, Ma'am?" A tractor trailer then pulled up in front of the building where they were standing, and the noise prevented Rachel from clearly hearing what the soft-spoken woman who stood before her was saying.

"Yes. I've been sent to retrieve a package from you."

"What did you say?" Rachel said with squinted eyes.

"I'm sorry. I said that I've been sent to retrieve a package from you. My employer said that you would have it."

"Really? And who is your employer?" Rachel asked curiously.

"Ms. Vandelyn, I've been given explicit instructions to retrieve the package with no questions asked or answered. I don't know what this is all about and, to be honest, it makes me nervous. I apologize for any concern you must have, but please just give me the package so that I can get it to him quickly?"

"Hmm...How can I be sure that you're who you say you are? I can't just hand something so valuable over to a person that I don't even know—that would be so ludicrous?"

Fear overcame Rachel as she tried to fathom what was now happening to her... standing here on the corner, surrounded by the noise of the street, not knowing if a gun was now being aimed in her direction from any one of these buildings.

"Ms. Vandelyn, I can assure you that I am the one that was sent to meet you. He said it is a box of jewelry that was left by your Aunt Myra. He said that your brother Devin told him about it. He also said that it is a matter of life and death. If I could get out of doing this, believe me, I would. But I can't. Please just hand it over so that I can return to him. I want to get this over with just as much as you do."

The tension was building as Rachel found herself pleading with the woman. "But my brother said I was supposed to give it to him."

"Please," Mildred said in desperation. "I must return with the jewelry."

Shaking her head, Rachel said, "No...no...no...Please, just let me think about this for a minute." She got ready to go to the car and ask Devin about it but the tracker trailer still sat there and traffic steadily moved, blocking her path.

"I must leave, Ms. Vandelyn. He's waiting for me to get back," said Mildred with tears in her eyes.

Rachel knew that they were in danger, and honestly felt sorry for the little woman who stood before her and said, "I guess you are who you say you are. I thank you for your kindness. This jewelry is precious to me and I am fearful of handing it over to a complete stranger. This is hurting me so much," she said with a strained voice. "But I guess it's something that I must do." Rachel paused, opened the flap to look at the box for the very last time and then said, "Okay...here...take it."

"Thank you, and I'm really sorry about this, Miss."

The woman took the package, held it tightly against her chest and hurried away. Rachel stood there watching with tears flowing as the woman got into the waiting car and rode away with Aunt Myra's jewelry. When she finally made it through the traffic to Devin, he asked, "Where is it? Where's the jewelry?"

"She has it?"

"She who?"

Angrily, she said, "Devin, didn't you see the lady that walked up to me when I came out of the bank?"

"No. With the traffic and trucks blocking my view, I couldn't see a thing."

"You know how safe it makes me feel to know that you weren't even watching out for me, Devin!"

Looking up in the air and rolling his eyes, he said, "but, Rachel, I told you how…"

"Devin, listen! She was sent to pick up the jewelry and wouldn't even give me his name, but said he was her employer. She knew all about you and what was happening so I gave it to her. So just shut up and let me process all of this. I am so upset right now and having a hard time accepting the fact that I just turned over my Aunt's jewelry to a complete stranger just because of your asinine behavior. Just shut up…leave me alone and take me home. Now!"

Devin quietly drove away, unsure of what he was to do next. The jewelry was gone. Was it over? Would his wounds have time to heal before his attacker returned? His stomach turned sour as he thought of possible scenarios.

# CHAPTER 15
## A Dinner Date

A fter a long, hot bath and time to calm herself, Rachel was finally able to get away from home. She met Trevor at the Parliament Restaurant. This was an upscale restaurant with a nice, romantic atmosphere. Chandeliers graced the ceiling of the historic building which courted the hearts of art and architecture enthusiasts. It was Rachel's first time at the restaurant. She marveled at the Grecian works of art as she entered the establishment in the downtown business district.

Trevor and Rachel were escorted to a secluded table in the far left corner of the massive room. She was a bit nervous as Trevor gently gripped her hand and helped her to be seated. Soft jazz music was being played by the house band as the waiter took their orders. The two of them then settled back, relaxed and conversed in small talk as they waited for dinner to be served.

Rachel uttered with a soft voice, "Trevor, this is such a beautiful place. How did you ever find it?"

He stared intently into Rachel's hazel eyes and admired her round face, framed by her naturally curly, black hair. *She is so beautiful,* he thought. His detective senses had taken over and in the annals of his mind, he was taking a photograph of her without the use of a camera. *I don't want to forget this beautiful picture of a woman who sits here in front of me. Thank you, God!*

Rachel felt a little embarrassed by the way he stared at her, but, at this moment, it made her feel like she was the most important person in the world.

"Trevor, I asked how you found this place," she said a little louder.

"Oh, I'm sorry…I just can't take my eyes off of you," he said in a voice that almost melted Rachel all over her seat. Rachel was glad that the lights were dimmed in the room; this would prevent him from seeing how much she was really blushing.

Finally answering, he said, "We had the policeman's ball here a year ago. Since that time, it's been one of my favorite spots. I love the architecture and it's so warm and inviting. I usually bring a book or magazine to read."

Rachel folded her hands underneath her chin and drew in closer to Trevor and said, "You really bring a book and read while you're eating here? You can't be serious. It's too romantic."

Trevor picked up on the signals Rachel was giving. He leaned in even closer and said, "Well, when you don't have company, that's what you do. I guess that's the life of a bachelor. It doesn't seem to bother anyone."

"Are you saying that you'll never get married?" She coyly said.

Trevor stared into Rachel's eyes with even more intensity. *Oh, dear God, he's doing it again.* She felt the warmth in her face return as he said, "Oh no; not at all. One day I'd love to get married to the right person that God sends my way...only time will tell."

Realizing how flirtatious she was being, Rachel sat back and shouted in her mind, *He believes in God! This could possibly be my husband!* She wasn't used to this type of exchange. She felt awkward and yet excited, all at the same time. She really wanted to make a gracious exit so she could renew her mind and gather her thoughts, but she sat there contemplating what to say next. She had to tone it down before she really gave him the wrong impression about who she was.

Trying to change things around, she said, "It's been a rather long and stressful day and it feels good to be here with you. The atmosphere and the music are calming."

"I'm glad you're here with me, Rachel. Would you like to dance, beautiful lady?"

Rachel gasped. "Um...Oh...no, I'm not much of a dancer...I can't dance at all. I have two left feet."

"Come on...you'll be just fine. Follow my lead," he said, standing and offering his hand to her.

Reluctantly, Rachel took Trevor's hand as he escorted her to the dance floor. His hand felt so good to Rachel. His hold was firm but soft at the same time. Other couples swayed and moved to the rhythm and the beat of melodic arrangements played by the band on the balcony-like stage. After a few moves, Rachel felt comfortable within his arms.

*This is nice and he smells so good*, she thought as his warm breath played upon her bare shoulder, enticing her as they danced close and intimately.

"See. It's not that bad," said Trevor as they moved across the cherry wood framed dance floor.

"No....it's not," she said in a near whisper. Every emotion that once lay dormant within the very core of her being was now stirred up as their bodies gently pressed together. The scent of his cologne and every movement he made tantalized her mind. She tried hard to arrest and not embrace the excitement that was overtaking every part of her body. Lustful emotion was now in charge.

From the bar, Michael Stern watched Rachel and Trevor as they danced across the floor. Lust was also playing in his mind as he thought about Rachel and how he could take her away from his nemesis, Devin.

Rooney, a drink mixologist—a term given to all of his bartenders by the owner—interrupted his thoughts. But this was only temporary.

"Mr. Stern, here's a sample of the new wine that was just brought in from the coast earlier today."

As he sampled the wine, he kept his eyes focused on the couple thinking, *Rachel Vandelyn, you will be mine. I can't let your heart be embraced by another man before my time. It's just the beginning. Things are about to change for you...hmm...and for me.*

"Mr. Stern, what do you think about the wine? Is it good enough for the Parliament?"

"Yes, Rooney...nice bouquet. Put it on the new wine list."

"Thanks, Mr. Stern."

"Rooney, see what table number 4 in the far right corner is having for dinner and send complimentary wines to their table. Let them know it's from the owner of the Parliament, but don't give them my name."

"Right away, sir."

Rachel was continuing to feel warm within Trevor's arms as the low melodic rhythm of the jazz band played. Wanting a way out of what she was feeling, she didn't want to offend him by letting go too soon. Looking towards their empty table, she found the perfect opportunity when she saw the waiter rolling a tray to their table.

"Oh, Trevor...look, the waiter is back with our food. We'd better hurry back and eat before it gets cold."

She quickly detached herself and made her way to the table. Already seated when Trevor returned, he said, "I must say, that was a quick exit."

Searching for an excuse, Rachel said, "I'm sorry. I just haven't danced in so long. I'm really not that comfortable on the dance floor."

"Well, I couldn't tell…no toes smashed here…you did well." In his mind, Trevor was regretting that their food came out so soon.

Rachel tried to soften the blow and said, "I'm ravenous and this food smells delicious. I had to take care of some personal business and missed eating lunch today."

Still feeling that he was thinking about what she did, Rachel said, "I hope I didn't offend you by leaving you on the dance floor; please understand, Trevor."

"Well… that's okay. I'm just licking my wounds… thought maybe I stepped on your toe or something, the way you quickly left me standing there."

"No. It's just me…nothing you did."

As she removed the silver dome food cover, Rachel said, "Mmm…This looks so good."

Sitting in front of her was a beautifully dressed salmon with cucumbers and a side of fresh sliced tomato, dappled with olive oil, salt and pepper. Trevor uncovered his seared scallops with spring onion and tarragon cream. After silently praying over her meal, she took her first bite when she realized that Trevor was watching her once again.

"How's your food, Trevor?" Rachel asked.

"I haven't tasted it yet. I was hoping we could bless our food together. We can just hold hands and pray silently. Are you okay with that? Although she had already prayed over her food, this was a surprise to her and caught her off guard. She agreed, put her fork down, and said, "I have no problem with a praying man." They then joined hands and with bowed heads, they prayed. She waited for him to say "Amen."

"Alright...let us eat, drink and be merry," said Trevor as he cut into his food. "Did I tell you how lovely you look this evening?"

"No, but thank you," said Rachel, feeling a bit shy and intimidated, knowing that he had his eyes on her while she ate. It had been some time since her last real date and having a man compliment her in this manner. It was hard for her to grasp the idea that someone could possibly have any interest in her. The note from Aunt Myra was a deciding factor for this date night. It was time to have some fun and enjoy life.

Two small bottles of wine were brought to the table by Rooney. "Sir and Madame, here are bottles of wine to complement each of your dinners. The bottles are sent to you as a gift from the owner of the Parliament.

"Oh, how nice. It will go beautifully with my salmon," said Rachel.

"Yes. Tell him thank you very much," said Trevor. "That was nice of him... guess he must recognize me from the police athletic league. Here, let me pour your glass, Rachel."

"Thank you. This salmon is delicious."

Trevor paused to take a bite from his own plate and then asked, "How are things coming along with settling your aunt's estate?"

"Okay," she said, but then Devin and his escapade suddenly resurfaced in her mind. She wished with all of her heart that she could tell Trevor what had transpired within the last four hours with Devin. She desperately needed to remove it from her mind as she didn't want it to ruin her dinner date.

"Trevor, I'm just trying to get beyond it and be free in my mind."

"I'm hoping I can really help you with that, Rachel. What kind of entertainment do you like? I see you don't like dancing. So what else is there? Do you like movies, ice skating? What is it that I can do to make life pleasant for you?"

"Trevor, you are hilarious. Right now, I really don't know what I like. I've been somewhat of a hermit for most of my life. So I really don't know what I like. Besides, this is our first date and it doesn't mean that there will be others."

Surprised by her comment, Trevor sadly said, "Oh… I thought things were going pretty well tonight."

"They are…I'm enjoying your company."

"Well then...okay...so it has to mean that you're willing to give this relationship a try?"

"Relationship?"

"Well, you know what I mean. Don't you want to see where we can go from here? The first time I saw you I—"

"Trevor, I really like you. But can we please— let's just take it slow. Okay?"

"Alright, Rachel. We'll take it slow, I'll give you time to see what a really nice guy I am."

Laughing, they ate their meal, enjoyed an amazing chocolate dessert with strawberries on top and most of all, they enjoyed each other's company before he took Rachel back home. There was no invitation into her home—just a kiss on the cheek and a goodnight hug. Time would have to be on their side in getting to know each other better.

# CHAPTER 16
## Dangerous Entrance

The next morning, Rachel was up early. Dreaming about her date with Trevor turned into a nightmare of horror when Devin showed up in her dreams with danger lurking all around him. His actions overruled a peaceful night. It awakened her, causing a restless affair with sleep. So she decided to get up, have breakfast, and take a walk in the cool breeze of the beautiful morning sun. She was hoping a walk along the trail that was attached to her home would clear her mind of his devilment.

Locking the door tightly behind her, she walked down the marble stairs and made her way across the beautifully manicured lawn, catching a whiff of lilacs that graced the front of her property. She hoped that on this morning, she would also be able to see a glimpse of the red Scarlet Tanager that was a frequent visitor to a bird feeder on the patio of her big white house which sat on the hill.

Rachel began to pray and meditate on one of her favorite scriptures, Jeremiah 29:11. *Lord, I'm feeling anxious and I know this is not Your will. Thank you for this lovely day and Your word which reminds me that You are a loving God, an awesome Abba Father who wants nothing but the best for me. You have great plans for me; plans to prosper me. Help me to see those plans and the provision you have for those plans. Help me to be a blessing to others as You create opportunities for me to live out those plans. And Lord, help me to love my brother the way You would want me to. Help me to be Your example, despite those times when I get scared, frustrated and annoyed. Bless him and continue to help us, Lord, in Jesus' name; Amen.*

A real peacefulness began to overtake Rachel as she walked along the trail. The further she walked, she began to see others who were also taking advantage of the early morning sun-filled day. Some walked, while others were running with their leashed dogs.

As she made her way, she thought about life and its destiny if something didn't change: *I have to let go of this pain I'm feeling. It's been so real within me and has overtaken everything. I can't continue to hold on to it. It's time to let it go. I want to live and have a little enjoyment in life. Besides, I'm not getting any younger. I really enjoyed my date with Trevor last night. I want to do more of that. God intends for His children to be free from bondage — any type of bondage. Lord, thank You for renewing my mind and helping me to enjoy this season of my life. Help me to gain wisdom... Your wisdom, as I get to know him better.* A smile made its way to the corners of her lips as she thought about the dinner and especially the dance with Trevor.

Not paying attention to where she was walking, her foot got entangled in a tree root that was protruding from the ground, causing it to twist as she fell to the ground. Intense pain permeated her ankle as she tried picking herself up in a lady-like manner. There was no one around that could help in her distress. Tears burned her eyes as she tried holding them back. Finally standing, she steadied herself back to her feet as pain gripped her body. She reached into her pocket and realized that she had forgotten to bring her cell phone. "What am I going to do now? God, please help me!"

She was suddenly startled at the rustling of trees behind her. A sense of relief gripped her as she came face to face with the handsome stranger who now stood in front of her.

"Are you okay, Miss?"

Even though she was relieved that he was there, she was a bit leery of his sudden appearance. She didn't know this man who would ultimately be her knight in shining armor—he was the only one present who could rescue her from this painful situation.

"Your knee is bleeding. Are you okay?"

Rachel was unaware that she was also bleeding. Her concentration was directed at the pain her ankle was causing each time she tried taking a step.

Reluctantly, she said, "Sir, can you help me? I tripped over that root sticking out of the ground and I'm having trouble walking. I need to get home and ice it before it swells up. I'm sure it'll be okay once I get home and elevate it."

Smiling within, he said, "Sure…I can help you."

Taking a handkerchief from his pocket, he wiped the blood from her knee. Rachel leaned on him as she struggled to keep her balance. He slowly walked away with her, smiling inside as he thought how lucky he was to be helping this damsel in distress make her way up the trail back to her home.

# CHAPTER 17
## Dangerous Revelation

Rachel leaned on the strong arm of this handsome stranger who helped her. As she took her last step to her front door, she felt relieved to finally be home.

Standing before the door, she suddenly stopped, not wanting to go any further. Her next move of opening the door would let this man, whom she did not know, in her personal space. Although he had so graciously taken the time to assist her, she still did not know him or his name. Turning the key would allow him access to her haven of safety and intrude upon the comfort of her home.

*How did this happen? What was I thinking?* The pain she felt prevented her mind from being the usual, sensible, well-guarded person that she was raised to be. Aunt Myra's voice was heard in her mind saying, *"Never talk to a stranger...be careful of who you let into your house...Never leave yourself alone in a situation with a stranger."* At a very young age, these were the words of wisdom her aunt and others who were important in her life taught. Now she was faced with a new dilemma. *Do I let him in or leave him standing here behind a closed door?* This man, who had no name, walked her ever so gingerly back to her home after her fall in the park. *God! Now he knows my address. Should I let him in? Help and protect me, Lord.*

Putting pressure on her foot was a great struggle and she needed someone to help her get inside. Anita was away for a family reunion in Bermuda so she would be alone for the next few days. *What should I do?* Hesitantly, she placed the key into the lock. He stood there watching her intently. Rachel was sure he could see the fear that was now all over her as her hand shook when she placed it there.

Before turning the key, she slowly faced him and said, "Sir, you have been so gracious to me and I don't even know your name."

"I also didn't get your name, beautiful lady. My name is Michael…Michael Stern."

Watching Rachel's every step that morning, it was his luck to see this mishap occur, and he planned to take every advantage of it. When he saw her with Trevor in his restaurant the night before, he also had a sleepless night as he thought about Rachel and how he would make his grand entrance into her life. Taking away her aunt's jewelry was just the beginning. He had a plan—a devious one that would end up hurting Devin. He want-ed his revenge and it would happen if it was the last thing he did. Just as Devin had taken the life of his sister, he would take Rachel from Devin in a very subtle manner. In Michael's mind, it was all meshing together perfectly.

"Now, I've told you my name. What's yours?" He said with a crooked smile.

Hesitantly she said, "Rachel."

"Rachel, if you don't mind, I'd like to make sure that you are able to get into your home safely."

"No, that's not necessary, Mr. Stern...You've done enough. I can make it from here."

"Please, call me Michael. And I wouldn't be a proper gentleman if I were to leave you trying to maneuver your way inside without my help."

Pure panic exploded within Rachel. Her heart pounded fast as her mind raced a quick marathon to find excuses as to why it was not possible to let that happen. She had to get this man away from her; he was now invading her place of refuge. Fear began welling up in her mind. *What am I going to do now? What have I gotten myself into?*

Holding back tears from both the pain she was feeling and now the fear of being hurt by this total stranger, Rachel began praying silently asking God to remove her from this desperate situation that she had so boldly entered into. *Father God, please help me. I need You now. Oh God, I don't know what to do.*

Beep...beep. A car horn was blaring and suddenly pulled up into her driveway. Turning away from the door, Rachel breathed a great sigh of relief and silently gave thanks to God when seeing her cousin, Delia, pull up in her red Nissan Maxima. Excitement embraced her mind as she thought, *God answers prayers after all... and all the time. Thank You for the reminder of Your faithfulness, Lord. Thank You!*

Looking back at Michael, she could see a hint of disappointment in his face as he also looked and saw that she now had company.

"Mr. Stern, I really don't need your help now. My cousin is here and she's more than capable of helping me. I really do appreciate all that you've done to get me back home. Thanks again."

"Well...I guess you're right. It was nice meeting you. I'm more than sure that we'll meet again and very soon, Ms. Vandelyn."

With these words, he quickly made his exit.

"Hey, cuz...." Delia said as he fled quickly past her, brushing against her shoulder. "Who's that disrespectful guy? Nice looking, but he didn't even acknowledge my presence? What kind of mess is that?"

"I'm sorry, Delia. Can you help me?"

Seeing Rachel grimace with pain with tears now rushing down her face, Delia ran up the stairs and holding onto Rachel she said, "Girl, what happened to you? Your knee is bleeding."

Rachel turned the key in the lock and opened the door with Delia's help. She was safe now and anxious to get inside to nurse her wounds. She was thankful to God for his intervention. Leaning on Delia, she explained her predicament and how she was so glad to see her drive up. "Rachel! How could you let a total stranger into your space like that? Have you lost your daggone mind? Don't you remember what Auntie taught you and even your own mother when she was sober? I can't believe you did such a crazy thing. My God...now that man, who you don't even know, has your address."

"I know...I know, Delia, but at that moment, I had no phone and no way of contacting anyone. I was in so much pain, I couldn't help it and it seemed like he just came out of nowhere—like a guardian angel...my knight in shining armor."

"You could have screamed for someone, Rachel. That was no knight in shining armor; he seems kind of suspicious to me. Please watch yourself. Be careful from now on. Thank God I came when I did. Here, sit down and let me put these pillows under your leg so we can elevate that ankle. And then I'll get some alcohol and bandages for the scrape on your knee and ice for the swelling."

While Delia got the ice, Rachel lay there and could not help but think about all that had happened. She couldn't shake his last words to her before he left, "I'm more than sure we'll meet again very soon, Ms. Vandelyn." The look in his eyes sent a chill through her and was something that she could not forget. *He was so confident...maybe it's nothing,* she thought as she rested her head on the arm of the chair.

Suddenly, she sat straight up realizing that there was more to this encounter than she could fathom. "How did he know my last name? He called me Ms. Vandelyn? He knows my name..." Fear sent a chill that was so intense — she couldn't shake it. She grabbed a shawl that was lying on the arm of the chair and cuddled in it.

Delia returned and nursed her wounds.

***

The next day, Rachel got up and again soaked her ankle in warm water concentrated with Epsom Salt. She was feeling a little better and was able to finally put some pressure on her injured foot. Alone in the house, a nervousness set in.

She could not get the face of the stranger out of her mind. "Who is this Michael Stern? I've got to get some information on him." Looking through her contact list, Rachel found the number she needed and began dialing. She waited patiently to hear his voice on the other end.

"Danison Detective Agency. This is Trevor, may I help you?"

"Yes...you can."

"Rachel?"

"Hello, Trevor."

"Wow. It's so nice to hear your voice again. I've left more than a few messages, but you never returned any of them. Honestly, I thought I'd done something to offend you at dinner and wouldn't hear from you again."

"No Trevor...no offense. I'm sorry. It wasn't you; it's me. I've got dating issues that need to be worked out on my own. I enjoyed being with you...Really I did."

"Well, that's good to hear. I enjoyed being with you too, but if it's a man issue and the way that some of us act...Rachel, I'm not that man. You don't have to worry about me getting out of line with you. I wouldn't dare rush you into anything you're not ready for." His voice was sincere, genuine and always had a mesmerizing effect on Rachel.

"Trevor...I know you wouldn't. I'm just—"

"That's okay, Rachel...You don't have to explain anything. I'm here for you when you need me. If you ever need a dinner partner, call me. You've got my number. I'd really like to take you out again, but only when you're ready."

"Thanks for understanding, Trevor."

There was an awkward silence for one quick moment and then Trevor said, "So, Rachel, why the call?"

Quickly she said, "Can you come over later?"

*So now she wants me to come over...okay God...I can handle this*, thought Trevor as he tried to contain his frustration with Rachel.

"Sure. Is everything okay?" he said hesitantly.

"If you'll come over, I'll be able to explain much better."

Curiosity was now eating at him and he said, "Well...I
only have two appointments this evening. I should be
finished around six. Is that soon enough?"

"Yes, that'll be great. Thanks, Trevor."

Hanging up the phone he thought, *What is it going to
take for her to trust me? I'm not going to be able to hold on to
hope much longer. Life is too short. I really don't have time for
this nonsense. But on the other hand, she's such a gorgeous
woman and if it's meant to be, I know that things will begin to
happen for us. What God has for me, is for me.*

# CHAPTER 18

## Devin's Unusual Lesson

"Where am I? Aarghh! My head is killing me."

Devin held his head and gently massaged his temples, trying to find relief from the extreme pain. "How did I get here?"

Finding himself lying on the ground, passed out in a dark alley, Devin could smell his own vomit. Reaching up and holding on to a large trash container, he slowly steadied himself to stand. The stench of garbage around him caused him to gag and vomit even more on his already damp clothing. He almost fell back to the ground.

Devin then reached into his back pocket and pulled out a crumpled Kleenex and wiped his mouth. He also discovered that his pockets were now empty...no phone, no wallet, and no keys. He could only surmise that he had been robbed and dumped in the alley, but he had no memory of what happened. The only thing he had to memorialize what he had been through was the pain in his head. Struggling for some memory, he could only bring back sitting in a bar and listening to jazz music at Jake's Hideaway on Route 38.

He was finally able to stand without falling and walked toward the alley entrance to see if he could get a visual of where he was. Although his steps were still a bit unstable, he was able to make it to the corner without falling.

"Randall Street. I have to get my bearing. I don't even know this street or its location—I have to get some help. My car!! Where's my car? It's gone. Whoever dumped me here must have taken my car!"

Devin felt even sicker and felt like he wanted to pass out, but shook the feeling by bending over and taking a deep breath.

He felt better, stood up and looking toward each corner, he searched for some sign of life on the narrow street. *This is so eerie*, he thought, as he made his trek down the quiet, dark and lonely street. He walked toward the light and noticed the beautifully detailed architecture of old constructed duplexes along the way. They were charming old buildings, each with its own nuance.

A store or a restaurant was now the only thing he had on his mind. He needed to find one that was open. One block... two and then three blocks passed, until he finally came upon a small café that was dimly lit and nearly empty. Looking through the plated glass window, he could see a few people sitting at oval shaped tables that were covered with red tablecloths.

Right over the glass windows a bright, flashing neon sign seemed to be the only sign of any life on the quiet block.

*The Arc Cafe...Hmm. It must be around closing time, but I have to get in and find a phone. Maybe there's someone here who can help me or even give me a lift, but with the way I smell, that is probably going to be a very slim chance of happening.*

As he entered the establishment, he felt the stares and heard the whispers when he walked over to the bar and sat down. Standing there was a tall, black man who looked to be in his late thirties, with dreadlocked hair down to his waist. As Devin sat down, the man locked eyes with him and said, "Mr., I'm sorry, but there's no way I'm going to serve you an alcoholic drink tonight. You look like you've had your fill and more. Sorry, I just can't do it. If you're looking for a meal, the kitchen is closed, but I can get you a snack...As for a drink, we have fruit punch, orange drink and seltzer water, sir, but no alcohol for you tonight."

"Listen, I'm not here for a drink. Can you just tell me where I am? How far am I from Delano Street?"

"Delano? Where's that?"

"It's on the east side of Route 38."

As he talked, the man cleaned the counter in front of Devin. "Route 38? I see...that's in the ritzy section of town. Man, it's at least 50 miles away. Did your GPS lead you in the wrong direction or break down or something?"

Shaking his head in disbelief, Devin said, "No...I'm really not sure what happened to me. I think someone may have robbed me and dumped me in the alley down the street. I don't even know where I am...I need help."

"So you think someone robbed you? Hmm..."

"I don't know. My head is killing me, I smell like vomit and I don't know what happened. . . I woke up in the alley and that's the only thing I'm thinking must have happened."

Leaning backward, the bartender said in a strained voice, "Yes, you do have a strong quality of smell permeating from your body."

With that comment, the entire bar exploded in laughter.

"I mean...you have been drinking. Haven't you?"

"I guess."

"Do I need to call the police?"

Hesitating, Devin said, "No ...no...I need to get myself together and think about this."

"Well, if someone robbed and stole your car, why wouldn't you want to call on the authorities to handle it?"

Devin was at a loss for words. His memory had failed him at not knowing what had happened and how he got to where he was. His habitual drinking had now landed him in a place where he had never been... this was too deep for him to even understand.

"Why?" Shaking his head in frustration, he said, "Because I can't remember anything! Can't you help me? Please."

Jeremiah Stone, owner of The Arc Café, could not help but feel compassion for Devin. He alone knew what it was like to be Devin's shoes; it was his past story — his life. Now, he was one who could not bear seeing others down on their luck — he rarely said, "No." His patrons loved him and enjoyed being around him at the café.

"Phew...that smell! Something's got to be done with you...or you'll send the rest of my patrons away from here because of it."

Leaning over the counter to talk privately to Devin, he looked him in the eyes and said, "First of all, sir — "

Interrupting him, Devin said, "My name is Devin Vandelyn...and yours?"

Softly he said, "Jeremiah Stone. I'm the owner of this establishment and you, sir, can't go anywhere smelling as you do." Looking to his right he yelled, "Mellie!!"

At the call, a heavy set, older black woman came rushing over to the bar. "Yes, Jeremiah...wah ya want?"

Jamella Gordon, lovingly called Mellie, was a God-fearing, Jamaican woman with a thick patois accent. Jeremiah was like a son to her and when he opened the café, Mellie was the first person he hired. With her help, customers filled it and became like a second family to

Jeremiah. He depended upon her to take care of the day-to-day operations of The Arc.

With a hardcore exterior, It wasn't easy for Mellie to trust anyone from a first meeting. Once she got to know you, there was nothing like her loving friendship. She had a heart full of compassion.

Whispering to her and Devin, he said, "Mellie, can you help this gentleman? Look in the worker's room and give him a set of clothes from the closet so he can change. He looks to be about Johnny's size and height, so give him a set of his clothing. I'll replace them later. Please show him where the shower is."

"Wah ya name?"

"Devin."

Shaking her head, with a hand on her hip, Mellie looked him up and down saying, "Aright Mr. Devin...Cum wid me, but jus keep you distance cuz you smell stink."

"Mellie!" Jeremiah frowned.

"Me jus saying..."

"Thanks, Jeremiah," said Devin, as he walked away following Mellie.

Jeremiah Stone watched as he left. Looking up, he said to himself, *Don't worry, God...I've got him...This one won't get away from you!*

# CHAPTER 19
## Passionate Planning

Michael Stern sat in his office thinking about Rachel and was still angry that his opportunity was hindered by an unwelcome guest. *I had her right there in the palm of my hands and then that broad showed up,* he thought as he shook his head in dismay. *There must be a god on her side. The way that car pulled up…right in the nick of time…hmm. Tonight, I'm going to have her. Devin is not going to get away with what he did to my baby sis. I just can't let it happen…I won't.*

With his mind made up, Michael strategized. He didn't care what it took to get back at Devin. His mission was to hurt him for what he did. Determination was eating away at him to avenge her death. Devin would suffer one way or the other.

He needed help for this one, so he called Jess.

"Hello."

"Jess, this is Stern."

"Hey, boss. I was just getting ready to leave town and take my mom back to Miami. What's up?"

"Before you go, I need you to take a look at the Vandelyn place again. Check out all the entrances and let me know what the best scenario is. I need a spot to get in and out quickly…got some business to take care of."

"If you want, I can take care of whatever business it is. I'm game."

"No, Jess. This one is mine, all mine."

"Okay. I'll get right on it. I need a little adrenaline stirred up. It's going to be a long drive to Miami and the caffeine ain't gonna help a whole lot."

"Driving? Why not fly?"

Sighing he said, "Mom doesn't like it."

"Oh…I see. Well get on this before you venture out. Thanks!"

"No problem, boss. No problem at all."

Michael sat down and laid his head back on his lounging seat. He would prepare to settle a debt that was long overdue. Revenge was his and his alone. Satisfaction would come with the final judgment of Devin Vandelyn and he was ready for it to happen sooner rather than later.

# CHAPTER 20
## Surprising News

Delia entered Rachel's house performing a balancing act in one hand. She held tightly onto a bag of warm, glazed donuts, mail retrieved from Rachel's mailbox, a photo album, and two cups of hot green tea that rested in a paper cup tray in the other hand. She was a little nervous, not knowing how Rachel was going to react to her news. Still, she was determined to hide her concerns from Rachel as she carefully sat everything on the kitchen counter.

As she arranged the tea and donuts on the table, she called out, "Rachel, I brought you some green tea and your favorite glazed donuts."

"I'm in the office. I'll be right there, shouted Rachel.

Delia went to the cabinet and pulled out a dessert plate for each of them and repeated over and over again in her mind, *It's going to be alright…it will…it will.*

Walking into the kitchen, Rachel smelled the delicious aroma of the sweet bread. "My mouth is salivating for those oh so yummy donuts." Hugging her cousin, she then reached into the bag and pulled out a glazed donut and sat it on her plate. "Mmm...and they're still hot. Did you get these from Brooks' Donuts?"

"I certainly did."

Licking her fingers, she said, "Okay, Delia...what's up? Why are you really here?"

"Can't I visit my favorite cousin when I want? Do I have to have an ulterior motive?"

"Well, no...I guess not...especially when you bring in a bag of my favorite donuts."

Delia took a big bite of her donut and then a sip of tea. As she savored the flavors in her mouth, she contemplated how she would share her news with Rachel.

Not looking at her, Rachel sensed that something major was on Delia's mind and said, "Delia, what's up? I can tell when there's something cooking in that brain of yours so just give it up. These donuts and tea have given me a peace that cannot be altered at this moment in time, so just say what's on your mind and get it over with."

"Okay...okay, Rachel. I do have something I need to tell you, but promise me you won't ruin what I have to say with the usual criticism? I'm happy about it and I don't want to lose my joy or regret anything because of the way you feel."

Rachel took another bite of her donut and between chews said, "Delia... What are you about to tell me? What have you done?"

"Rachel...promise me first."

"How can I make a promise when I don't have any facts yet? What is so serious that I have to make a promise? Please just go ahead and tell me."

Delia took a sip of tea, swallowed and said, "Okay...hmm."

Thinking about how to give Rachel the news, she jumped up from the table and went over to the kitchen counter and picked up a small photo album that was decorated with a little white lace bow and two dainty silver church bells centered on the top. Slowly walking over to Rachel, she handed the little book to her. Delia stood there like a little girl standing before her mother, waiting to be reprimanded for bad behavior.

"What's this?" Rachel asked, as she took it in her hand. First admiring the cover, she opened it and read the title page aloud. "The Marriage Album of Delia Vandelyn and Garry Briton? You're married? To Garry Briton? Delia! How could you after what he did to you?"

"Rachel, please. He's changed. It wasn't his fault!"

"Well whose fault was it, Delia? He walked out on you. I can't forget the night you waited for him and he didn't show. You cried like a baby and now you're telling me that you married that jerk! Delia!"

"Rachel, I need for you to be quiet and listen to me." Tears began to flow as Delia spoke with passion about her relationship with the man she truly loved.

"Garry has been back in my life for a few months now. He never wanted to leave me. It was his dad that caused so much heartbreak between the two of us. He kept feeding lies and all sorts of crazy things to Garry. He was even going to have me investigated and Garry stopped him from doing it to save me. His father...that wicked man, even tried to pay me off to stay away from his son. He told me if I left town and went to California he would pay for my airline ticket, take care of my living arrangements, and would even set me up with a record producer. He stipulated that I would have to promise not to call Garry or ever come back to this city. He did it, Rachel... it wasn't Garry. His father let the cat out of the bag on his death bed, Rachel...on his death bed! I love Garry and he loves me! We're married and that's all there is to it!"

Rachel was stunned at what she had just heard. Seeing the tears, she knew that Delia was serious about what she had just revealed. At this point, there was nothing more she could say that would change Delia's mind or make any difference, and Rachel knew it. All she could do was try as best she could to be happy for Delia. Standing up, she walked over to Delia and embraced her little cousin.

"I'm sorry, Delia. I didn't know. I just didn't know. If you're happy... I'm happy too!" Smiling at Delia, she said, "Where's my new cousin? I want to congratulate the two of you together…We'll have to get the family together and throw a dinner party for you."

Those encouraging words coming from Rachel made all the difference in the world. Embracing each other, Delia knew that everything would be alright. Her husband would be accepted by the rest of the family and they would love him the way that she loved him.

Stepping back from Delia, Rachel looked at her and said, "You're really happy?"

"Yes, I am."

"Well, I can see it and I'm happy for you, baby cuz. I'm glad you told me about this but please promise me that, if things don't work out the way you want, you won't hide it from me…promise me that?"

"Rachel, things are going to work out. Please believe me."

"Delia, either way…promise me."

"Okay, Rachel…I promise."

"Thank you. Now pass me that bag so I can get another donut."

Laughing, they finished up their treat and sat down to make plans for a family dinner that Rachel would host in Delia and Garry's honor.

# CHAPTER 21
## A Preconceived Notion

T alking with Trevor gave Rachel some semblance of peace knowing that with his help, she would find out who this Michael Stern was. After taking a long hot shower, she went into her closet to pick out something nice to wear before his arrival.

She thought back on her dinner date and remembered how she felt when they were dancing in each other's arms. The pressure of his body against her, the smell of his cologne, and his breath on the back of her neck made her once again burn with unrelenting desire. *Wow! I may need to jump back into the shower and turn on the cold water...got to get this sensuous feeling under control,* she thought, as she rambled through her walk-in closet.

Rachel finally decided on a Peony jersey with a one-shoulder neckline. After massaging with lotion, and a quick spritz of her favorite cologne–White Diamond–she went into the kitchen and prepared a light meal of salmon on salad greens with raspberry balsamic vinaigrette, croissants, and raspberry iced tea. For dessert, she had lemon pound cake, which she topped with whipped cream, shredded chocolate and strawberries.

"There. Everything is all set for his arrival. I didn't say we'd have dinner, but I'm sure he'll stay and enjoy it."

Not long afterwards, the doorbell rang. Trevor stood there with a dozen red roses in hand, smiling as Rachel opened the door.

"Trevor...It's so nice of you to bring flowers. They're beautiful," she said as she took a deep whiff of their scent."

"Please do come in."

"Beautiful roses for a beautiful lady," he said, as he entered and kissed her on the cheek.

Rachel felt herself blushing and hiding her face as she thought, *Okay, satan...what are you up to? He sure knows how to turn a girl on. Lord, help me!* She led him into the living room.

"I hope you're hungry, Trevor. I've prepared a light meal for us. I know you came straight from your office and probably haven't had a chance to eat. Have you?"

"As a matter of fact, no, I haven't. Thanks, Rachel."

"Go ahead and sit down at the table. I'm going to put these roses in a vase and I'll bring out your plate. There's raspberry iced tea in the pitcher with sliced lemons on the side. Go ahead and pour some for us. I'd like two lemons, please."

Rachel went into the kitchen and snipped the ends of the roses diagonally. She put them into the vase with cool water, two pennies and a teaspoon of sugar. She was told that flowers last longer with that concoction. Not sure whether it really worked or not, she always did it any- way.

Pouring their drinks, Trevor thought about Rachel and how pretty she was. *The scent of her cologne is enough to make any man want to jump right on that sexy babe. I'll wait...don't want to seem too anxious. I really believe that one day she'll give in to me, accept a marriage proposal and won't regret it...won't regret it at all.* As he placed the pitcher of tea on the table, Rachel came back with a serving tray of salads, croissants and butter.

Trevor watched Rachel's every move as she placed the roses in the center of the table. Then she walked over to him and put a dish of salad in front of him, followed by a saucer of two croissants, and a side of butter. She then placed her meal on the table. Rachel was well aware that Trevor was watching her so with each step, she gently accentuated her movements hoping that he would be captivated. What was he thinking now? Did she have some preconceived notion that she was now more ready than he was to be intimate? Had she played hard to get for too long? The game was over—she was ready to be taken. Then she felt a sinking feeling. *Am I really ready? Is this really who I am? I know what the word of God says. Do I believe it or not? I can't defile what God has placed within me?* Shaking her head as if she was disgusted with herself,

Rachel made her way into the dining room and tried to shake off what she was really feeling.

Sitting down at the small table, she placed the salt and pepper grinder, before him and said, "So how was your day?" Her hands were shaking. She hoped he wouldn't notice.

"What? I'm sorry, what did you say?" Trevor was pulled away from his sensuous thoughts and was brought back to reality by Rachel's question.

"I asked you how your day was."

"Oh...it was slow. I didn't realize how hard it would be to get started with this new business. I've gotten a few new clients, but not as many as I had hoped. My goal for each month is to get in at least two a day, but that's not happening. I hired a PR company and they're putting together a proposal for me that will help to get things moving in the right direction. Once the clients start coming in, I can hire staff."

"That's good. Do you regret leaving the police department?"

"No, not really. With the money my dad has given me, I'm set to do this. My bills are paid and I have no debt. So if things don't fall in line as quickly as I'd like them too, I'm still good."

"You're a man with vision. I admire you for that."

All Trevor could do was smile as he savored his food.

"Are you enjoying the meal? I'm not the world's greatest cook, but I can put a salad together in a heartbeat."

"Rachel, it's delicious. Really hits the spot."

"Thanks, Trevor."

Wanting to get to the point of her call, he said, "Now what did you need help with...What's going on?"

"Can we talk about it once we finish our meal and go to the sitting room?"

"Okay...if that's what you'd prefer."

"Yes, I don't want to lose my appetite thinking and talking about what is to come."

Curiosity filled Trevor's mind as he broke the salmon into little pieces on top of his salad greens.

# CHAPTER 22
## Devin's Revelation

Mellie handed Devin a loofah sponge, a bath towel, a brand new bar of shea butter soap and said, "Misa Devin, if it wus me, me wouldn't get out of da showa till I can smell da sweet breat of Gad. Me put some clean clothes ova de on da bench. Put ya dutty clothes inna da trash bag—unless ya plan on keepin dem."

"Oh, no thanks...You can just dump them. I appreciate it. Thanks, Mellie."

"Me a Ms. Mellie fe yu, Misa Devin. If an wen we get to know each odda betta, I'll tink about lettin yu call me by me fus name. Now put da lock on da door an tek ya showa, man."

"Sorry about that, Ms. Mellie."

Leaving the room, she walked away singing, "He's the lily of the valley. He's the bright and morning star. He's the rose of Sharon and He lives forevermore."

Devin felt anxious to get out of the soiled clothing. He locked the door and quickly removed the smelly, vomit-drenched clothing from his body and placed them into the trash bag. He was glad to finally get into the shower. The stench on his body made him feel so dirty and worthless. In his mind, he had to get the dirt off quickly. So with soap in hand and the loofah sponge, he began to scrub every inch of his body until he could scrub no more. Standing there naked, he allowed the water to flow freely over his body. In some way, it felt spiritual for him, like he was getting rid of all the dirt and mess he had caused in his life. So he stood there and let the hot water flow for a good while.

In the shower, he found a bottle of shampoo and began to pour it into his hair while massaging his scalp. Pain gripped his body when he found a large bump on his head and some dried blood. *This must be where they hit me. What happened to me? Why can't I remember what happened?* As hard as he tried, Devin could not remember any of what got him into that alley. His memory was lost. Everything was a blank.

*How am I going to explain to the police what happened if I can't even remember?* Scrubbing away, he thought, *Well, I guess it's good I don't have credit cards. There was a little cash in my wallet...don't remember how much I had, but there were a few dollars. My license expired with the old address on it.* Shrugging his shoulders, his mind was blank as to what he should do. What he did know was that something had happened to him and something had changed, but he couldn't put his finger on it.

"I've got to call Rachel...I've got to call my sister." Finally stepping out of the shower, he dried off and rushed to put on the new clothing. For Devin, this would be a long night.

# CHAPTER 23

## Trevor's Impassioned Appeal

A fter dinner, Trevor and Rachel headed into the sitting room for dessert and coffee, made with some of her favorite freshly ground Columbian coffee beans. Setting their cups and dessert on the table, she sat on the sofa with Trevor.

"Now, Rachel."

"Now what?"

"It's time for you to tell me why you really called me here today. What's this all about? I'm enjoying the pleasure of your company and excited about the fact that you even called me—especially after not acknowledging any of my calls or text messages. To be honest, I gave up on even thinking that you and I would be having any further contact with each other. I don't want to feel like you just call me whenever you have a problem or need an investigation. To be honest, Rachel, I really think I need to start charging you for my time and services."

Rachel chuckled, but soon realized that Trevor's demeanor had changed. The joy of his being there had suddenly waned.

"Rachel, I'm serious. Should I start treating you just like any other client and hand you a bill for my services? Tell me, Rachel. If that's all there is to it, just let me know."

Trevor's words cut Rachel to the core. He was right. She had played him one too many times and now he was hurt.

"Trevor...I'm so sorry you feel like this."

"Rachel, you have to come one better than that. Did you call me over here to fix another situation for you? If so, then let me get out my notepad to take down the information and give you a bill for my valuable time."

Burning tears began to well up in Rachel's eyes as the sharp darts of hurt flew from Trevor's mouth. This was painful, but she knew in her heart that he had every right to say and feel the way he did.

As Rachel turned her back to wipe away the tears that had now begun to trickle down her face, Trevor stood up and said, "Well, it's been nice, but I think I'd better leave now. If you need someone to help you with a problem, I'll send over a list of a few of my colleagues. They'll be more than happy to help you out."

The panic grew deep within Rachel as Trevor got up and walked away. She was at a loss for what to do or say, but knew she couldn't let him leave feeling the way he did. Now, more than ever, she knew she had to let the pain of her past hurts go. They had held her hostage and prevented her from letting any man get close. She had to let it go, once and for all.

Rushing toward him she said, "Trevor! Please don't leave me...Please stay with me! Don't leave yet, please. I need to explain!" With those words, Trevor turned back toward Rachel. Seeing her genuine pain and tear-filled eyes, he embraced her and held Rachel's trembling body in his arms and passionately kissed her. She was like a rag doll in his arms, succumbing to his warm body pressed tightly against her limp frame. The hurts of the past seemed to have slipped away and took her to a place of peace and new found feelings.

Trevor didn't want to let her go, but Rachel, not wanting to give into the passion she was also feeling, pulled away and looked up into his eyes and said, "I need to share some things with you. Here, come sit on the couch with me and let's talk."

Now Trevor really felt dejected and reluctantly let go. Taking him by the hand, they walked over and sat down.

"It really hurts me that you're thinking I'm using you. That really has not been my intent. Relationships—close relationships—with men have been hard for me."

Confusion fell upon Trevor's face and he asked, "Why, Rachel? You're such a beautiful woman. I fell for you the first day I saw you. It seems like every man would be constantly at your beck and call, trying to date you all the time.

"Maybe…but I have never given it a chance to happen."

Trevor seemed more confused than ever and said, "Rachel, I'm not understanding you. Where are you going with this? What happened to make you feel this way?"

Tears glistened in her eyes and, with a trembling voice she said, "Trevor, you seem like someone I can trust. Are you, Trevor? Are you?"

He could feel the sincerity in Rachel's words as she got up and began pacing the floor. His heart was breaking for her. She looked so vulnerable. He wanted to hold her so badly. But somehow he felt that would be premature. He needed to listen first and assure her that he was a man she could trust."

"Rachel, up to this point, have I done anything that would make you think that you can't trust me? I…I love you, Rachel. You're all I think about from the time I get up in the morning. You're always on my mind."

"Please, stop, Trevor! Just stop! How can you love me when you don't know what I've been through and what I've done!"

He could now see tears flowing from Rachel's eyes. It was taking every bit of endurance not to get up and embrace her. All he could do was pray, asking God, *What can I do? How can I help her if I don't know what she's really feeling and why she's even feeling this way? God! Help me to help her! Help me to understand!*

# CHAPTER 24

## Rachel Faces Her Past

Having to face Trevor and tell him about her past weighed heavily on Rachel as she sat next to him on the couch. Trevor felt somewhat helpless but, in his mind, he continued to pray asking God's favor and grace for the one he loved, hoping that she would open up and give him a chance to help her through her feelings.

As Rachel began to quietly think about the deep-seated hurt caused by her brother, uncontrollable tears began to flow as the pain of remembering the years she endured rape and degrading control as her body was taken by Devin. The thought of it made her feel sick and she curled up like a newborn baby on the couch.

Pleading with her, Trevor asked, "What's wrong, Rachel? Please, let me help you?" He moved closer to her on the couch.

"No, Trevor; it's not you. I was just thinking."

"Thinking about what?" he said, gently wiping the tears from her eyes.

"I really don't want to talk about it. . .not now."

"But why the tears, Rachel? You make me think I did something wrong. . . Did I say something to stir up pain? Rachel, please help me to understand what's going on here. You said that you wanted to explain something to me, so explain now…please?"

Rachel turned to Trevor, looked him in the eyes and shook her head. "Trevor, I want to but…I just can't…I — I don't want you to think any less of me. I just can't."

"Rachel, I won't think any less of you. Please just tell me and we'll work through it…together," he said as he gently kissed her forehead.

Rachel's body was now trembling as she spoke, so Trevor grabbed a blanket that was lying on the couch and covered her, thinking that she was cold. Her trembling was not from being cold, but it was from the fear she felt in losing him once he heard her story. She had strong feelings for Trevor; feelings she had not revealed because of her trust issues.

Finally giving into his pleading, Rachel said, "Okay…okay, but please don't judge me when you hear what I have to say."

"I won't, Rachel. Trust me. I won't."

Resting on his chest, but facing away from him, Rachel softly said in a quivering voice, "Trevor, from the age of ten, I was raped nearly every night by my brother.

He would come into my bedroom and take advantage of me. Each time, he would threaten to cut me open with a knife that he placed on the nightstand so I would lay there and take it. For years, I endured his abuse until one night I had the boldness to do something about it."

Trevor could not believe what he was hearing, but felt nothing but pity for Rachel. Wrapping his arms around her trembling body, he comforted her as she now cried uncontrollably.

In anguish and tears, she cried, "Trevor, the last night I allowed him to do his dirt to me, I beat him to the punch and took the knife and cut him…I cut him!"

He held on even tighter to Rachel as she turned, burying her face into his chest, and cried. Looking at this woman who was pressed into his body, Trevor felt so much hatred toward Devin. Shaking his head, he tried as best he could to hug the pain away from Rachel. In the back of his mind, he wanted to find a way to make Devin pay for all the pain he had caused this woman whom he loved. At that moment, he was determined to make Devin Vandelyn pay for his sins, but he knew that he couldn't let his emotions lead him.

Trevor released his hold on Rachel, lifted her chin and brushed away her tears as he said, "It's going to be okay, babe…it really will. I still love you, no matter what. This has not changed the way I feel about you and it never will."

Trevor sat with Rachel holding her until she fell asleep. The strain of it all had worn her down. He carefully laid her head on a pillow, locked the door and left her lying there on the couch. These feelings of wanting to physically hurt Devin were real and hard to deal with. He knew he'd have to find a way to release his anger. Praying was the only way.

# CHAPTER 25

Truth is Revealed to Michael

T ired, Michael Stern went to his wine cellar, got a bottle of Cabernet Sauvignon and retired to his bedroom. Getting the information he needed from Jess, he thought about what his next step would be. He was determined to get back at Devin no matter what the outcome.

It was his nightly ritual to sit on his bed, pour a glass of wine and read. Lately his reading material had been something that stirred his every emotion. It was the one and only reason he was so intent on getting his revenge on Devin. The readings came from his sister Melinda's diary. She loved writing and had accumulated over a dozen diaries. When she died, a box of her personal effects was recovered at the scene and was turned over to him. It was something that he had only recently been courageous enough to look through. Since her death, the diaries had been locked up in one of his wall safes.

At first, he was wary of opening up the pages. There was just something too personal about reading his sister's private thoughts that didn't seem right. Finally, after months of soul searching and mind boggling thoughts, he began reading. It was there in her writings that he really met Devin and found out who he really was.

Michael and Devin had never gotten an opportunity to meet personally when Melinda was alive. There was only one phone call made to Michael—forced upon Devin by Melinda. That call was to ask for Melinda's hand in marriage; it wasn't an ideal situation. At that time, Michael was living in California and working in Japan. They were not able to meet face to face. Melinda was anxious about him accepting Devin, so she made the call so that it would be done. She wanted to be comfortable with the situation and not feel like she was keeping any secrets from her big brother. Knowing how impatient his sister could be and, wanting only to make her happy, Michael gave his blessing by phone. He was not happy about it, but he did it anyway. In talking to him, Michael also gave Devin a warning that if he ever hurt his sister in any way, death would be his only wedding present. Although Michael was chuckling when he said it, he made sure that Devin knew how very serious he was and would make good on every threat.

Now, Michael sat on his bed with a drink in one hand and the diary in the other, reading night after night. His sister had many diaries, but this one was the one that led up to the marriage to Devin. Melinda loved Devin but there were moments, as Michael read through Melinda's private thoughts, that he questioned whether or not Devin really loved his sister. Tonight, he was on week three of the month of June, just seven days prior to their wedding day.

*"Dear Mr. Diary,*

*Today I just couldn't help myself. Help myself to do what? Well, I found the address for Devin's Aunt Myra and his sister Rachel. It's seven days before the big day and I'm going to surprise him by inviting them to the wedding. He's been adamant about not inviting them because he thinks that they won't come. Apparently there's been a lot of bad feelings and grief between them – especially with his sister, Rachel. He won't tell me what happened. He says it's in the past and won't give me any details about what happened to cause this rift between the two of them. He says it was years ago, so that shouldn't be an issue. Should it?*

*Anyways, I'm going over there today and introduce myself. I'm so excited about meeting the two of them. So let me go and I'll get back to you later, Mr. Diary."*

Turning to the next page, Michael smiled at his sister and how she addressed her writing as "Mr. Diary." She was such a sweet, child-like girl. He missed her so much. He continued to turn the pages, anxious to see what she had written next. How would this meeting go? How accepting would they be of his little sister?

"Dear Mr. Diary,

I'm back from my visit with Devin's aunt and sister. Come to find out, they live about an hour away. My GPS really worked for me today. I was a little nervous when I drove up to the house. It's a beauty. I love the way it sits back on the lush green grass. It's right next to a park! These people seem to really have some money! But that really means nothing to me. I was so nervous. When I rang the doorbell, this lady named Anita answered and took me to the living room where I waited for a little bit. Finally, both of them walked in and I introduced myself. At first they seemed a bit standoffish. But then as we began talking, Devin's aunt asked if I had lunch and since I had not eaten, she suggested that the three of us go to her favorite seafood restaurant, Captain Buck's, to eat. Once we got there, we ordered the buffet and talked, laughed and enjoyed each other's company.

Finally, I told them about the wedding. When I did, both of them looked at each other, stood up and embraced me. They were so excited about it! Sitting back down though, I could see some concern on the face of his sister, Rachel. She asked me if I was sure about getting married to Devin. I said, 'Of course...I love him so much and he loves me.' She smiled at me and said, 'Okay...If you're sure about it, I'm happy for you.' But then, Aunt Myra got up—Yes! She told me to call her Aunt Myra! So excited *about that! But anyways, Aunt Myra got up and excused herself to the ladies' room. When she left, Rachel seemed like she was trying to discourage me from marrying her brother by telling me how he can be. At first, I was a little perturbed that she was talking about him in that way. But she said that she was only trying to make sure for my sake that I really knew what I was getting into. It was all about her concern and care for me. I really like her. She is going to be the sister that I never had. I really, really like her!*

*Aunt Myra returned to the table and she and Rachel asked me what I needed for the wedding. Look at this...They just met me and are offering to help me! Rachel asked if I had the flowers all set. She has a friend who owns a flower shop and now she wants to pay for all the flowers. The only thing that I had as far as the flowers was my bouquet and one rose for each of my bridesmaids. Rachel told me to give her the name of my wedding planner and she is going to take care of everything else that I need. Look at that! I was going to ask Michael for help, but hesitated because I really didn't want to ask for my big brother's help. Now I don't need it! My new sister-in-law is going to see to it that I have everything I need! Wow! This has been a great day. Rachel told me to call her tomorrow so that we can meet up again! She's taking me shopping for honeymoon stuff! Good night, Mr. Diary!!!"*

Michael's eyes filled with tears as he realized that Melinda had bonded with Rachel. Rachel knew his sister and was trying to help her, not just with the wedding, but she also tried to warn her about Devin. How could he now do anything that would hurt her? He cried like a baby and drank the entire bottle of wine falling asleep in a drunken stupor.

# CHAPTER 26
## Devin Faces a New Reality

D evin tried calling Rachel several times but was unable to make any contact. Not wanting to leave a voice message, he hung up and decided to try again in the morning. He then called the local police department to report his stolen vehicle. With very little information to give, he didn't feel confident that there would be much success in getting his car back. It was a very frustrating call as he went back and forth with the operator who kept asking questions that he was not able to answer. The disappointment of not being able to get in contact with his sister and the aggravating call made to the police caused his bruised head and ego to feel even worse.

"What's the matter, my man?" Jeremiah asked as he dried the last few glasses at the bar.

"Oh, nothing…nothing at all," said Devin as he rubbed the painful spot on his head.

Jeremiah heard Devin when he was talking with the police department and sensed his frustration. He now saw it written all over his tired face. Trying to cheer him, he offered Devin dinner and a night's stay in a warm bed at The Arc Café, which also had a bed and breakfast on the upper two floors. Devin gladly accepted.

Sitting in the small dining room of the café, Devin began thinking, *What's happening? It's been a crazy day and I'm just tired of all this. What am I supposed to do now? I can't continue to go on like this. Family can't stand me...I have no friends...Rachel probably saw my name on the caller ID and just didn't pick up. Can't blame her after all I've done to ruin her life. I'm —*

"Devin! Where were you just now? I was asking if you wanted lemonade or sweet tea."

"I'm sorry...Sweet tea is good."

Jeremiah sat a plate of fried plantains, cabbage, red beans and rice with oxtails in front of him. As he set the tea down, Devin thanked Jeremiah and said, "Wow...this looks so good. What is it?"

Jeremiah smiled as he also handed him a room key and said, "Just eat, my man. It's good Jamaican fare. You'll love it."

Devin took more than a few bites, savoring each flavor and said, "Mmm...mmm...mmm. This is so good. Thanks so much."

"You're quite welcome. I'll have to let Mellie know that you love her cooking."

"Mmm…she's some cook. Please do tell her. I offend-ed her tonight by calling her Mellie instead of Ms. Mellie."

"Oops! I should have warned you that she's really particular about things like that. She has to warm up to you before she lets you get anywhere close. She's a good, loving person, though."

"I guess you'll have to prove that one to me."

"Well, once she gets to know you, there's no friend like Mellie."

"Oh really…"

"Yes! She's a good-hearted, Christian woman and will help anyone at a moment's notice. But do not, I repeat, do not make her mad. That Jamaican temper will flare so hot, you'll swear you can feel the heat of her wrath shooting right in your underwear like a spanking from your parents!"

Laughing, Devin said, "Okay, although it's a tad bit late, thanks for the warning." Jeremiah chuckled as Devin continued eating and enjoying his meal.

Finishing his work at the bar, he took a seat at the ta-ble with Devin and asked, "What are your plans, my man? I really believe there was a godly purpose for your presence here tonight."

"What do you mean—a godly purpose?"

"Come on, you know what I'm saying. There is a rea-son for everything that happens in this life. I believe in God and there is a scripture in Jeremiah, named after me, of course," he said with a grin, "that tells us how God has our path of life written down even before we're born. Your path led you here tonight to this café to meet me."

Devin sat back in his seat, picked up a napkin to wipe his mouth, and angrily threw it down on the table. After taking a sip of his sweet tea, he said, "Okay, now I have to hear about God and the Bible? Jeremiah, I'm sorry, but I'm just not into all of that. I don't have anything against people who do, but I'm not a good person and have no dealings with God. He probably wants nothing to do with me either, especially with the life I've lived. My life has been so jacked up. I've hurt so many people who were close to me in this lifetime that sometimes I can't even stand myself."

"Listen, Devin, just cool down."

Devin's voice was now raised. Jeremiah could see that, at that moment, he would not be able to calm this angry man.

Pushing away from the table and standing, Devin said, "Jeremiah, I'm trying to stay cool and I appreciate your hospitality, but please don't tell me what to do!!"

"Devin, I'm not going to force anything on you or try to tell you something that you'd rather not hear. But just think about it. You're here in The Arc tonight. You can't remember a thing about how you got into that alley, and you're sitting here with a licensed and ordained minister of God."

"You're a minister! Oh...so that's it! You think that just because you're a minister you can now preach to me!!"

Jeremiah remained calm. "Devin, I don't think that at all. It's not something that I publicly proclaim, especially since I run a bar. Some people would really look down on me for that. I look at it as my opportunity just to be where the hurt souls are. I like getting right down to where the hurt ones are."

Devin was upset and turned his back to walk away, but stopped and taking a deep breath, calmed down a bit as he asked, "What do you mean?" He turned back and faced Jeremiah.

Jeremiah stood to meet him and said, "Devin, look at my situation. I was an alcoholic who became a preacher. I started out in a regular, four-walled church building. I got no satisfaction in being closed up behind those walls. God changed that and now I'm here in a place where I get to meet all types of people. They come from all types of backgrounds and sit here before me at the bar, at the tables, and in the bed and breakfast rooms. I see the drunk, the prostitute, the adulterous man and woman, the liar, and the cheater. And because I am here, I can give a word of encouragement. With the help of God, they are convicted of right and wrong in this atmosphere. It's a place of familiarity and comfort for everyone who walks through those doors. I love that I get to meet personally with each of them on a regular basis. They have become like family, looking for me every time they come in here. Lives have been changed. They get through the hardships of life. God put me here for this purpose and I believe He sent you here. This is the day God has destined for you."

Devin looked at Jeremiah blankly, went back to the table and sat down, picked up his fork and continued eating.

"Okay, Devin. I can see you don't want to talk anymore right now. So we'll talk more in the morning." Jeremiah got up and locked the doors and turned down the lights. Before he walked away, he said, "Your room is on the third floor. Breakfast is served at 8 a.m. I'll see you then. Good night."

As Jeremiah walked away, Devin ate the last bit of his food angrily, but didn't say a word because he didn't want to offend his host by saying something that he would soon regret. There was no response, but in his mind he was thinking, *Sorry, Jeremiah, but you won't see me in the morning. I'll sleep here tonight, but at the light of day, I'm going to find a way back home if I have to beg, borrow or steal.*

# CHAPTER 27

## Michael's New Mindset

The next morning, as Michael showered, he could not help but think about the words he read in sister's diary the night before. When she said, *It was all about her concern and care for me. I really like her. She is going to be the sister that I never had. I really, really like her!* That really touched Michael. Although he was feeling the pain of his binge drinking, his mind was now clearer than ever. There had to be a new game plan.

Rachel was not his enemy—Devin was. There was no way he could point his finger at her and cause her any additional pain. She had befriended his sister. He now felt that he had to make things right with her by returning the stolen jewelry. But how was he to make that happen? Standing there, he knew that there were only two choices. Maybe he could mail it to her and hope that it would be received safely back into her hands. There would be no return address...Or he could merely have

Jess place it on the doorstep of her home. "Yes, that's what I'll do...I'll send Jess."

He quickly got out of the shower, almost stumbling out of the stall as dizziness overcame him. "Can't keep drinking like I did last night...not good," he said aloud as he held on to the sink which was adjacent to the shower.

Looking at his image in the large, rectangular mirror over the sink, a sickening feeling churned in his stomach as he asked himself, "Who have you become, Michael? Look at you. Are you a business man or have you become a thug who is out looking for some petty revenge?" Shaking his head, he could no longer bear to look at himself. He bowed his head in shame as the urge to vomit took over and he purged into the sink.

Brushing his teeth and rinsing his mouth he thought, *Things have got to change...I can't do this anymore...This is not my life. It's become an obsession.*

# CHAPTER 28

## Devin Has a Breakdown

D evin was up early the next morning. He didn't want to hear another word from Jeremiah or anyone else about God or what God had pre-destined for his life. So he was determined to leave before having to face anyone. *There is no way I can change now...all this crap about God...is there really a God?* Thoughts bombarded his mind like an uncontrolled whirlwind as he hurried to get away from The Arc.

"Misa Devin, wey yu goin?" Mellie was up early too—working in the kitchen prepping for breakfast. Surprised by her presence, Devin tried to ignore her as he hurried through the dining room.

"Misa Devin, me kno yu hear mi. Yu ansa me now and stop bein ignorant and rude. Ansa me now, man."

"It's time for me to leave and go home. I can't stay here another day."

"Misa Devin, wha yu runnin wey for? Yu can at leas eat breakfus. Mi mek a wicked bowl of grits, scrambled egg and biscuit wid hot maple sirup."

"Listen, I'm really not hungry," he said, shaking his head and trying not to show the anger that was spewing from his mouth.

"Aright—if yu sey so. How yu getting bak home, Misa Devin?"

Devin was not sure what he was going to do, but knew someway, somehow he would get back home. Surely, Rachel would come and get him. He believed in his heart that this time she would answer his call.

"Ms. Mellie," he said with his voice a little raised, "I have a sister, named Rachel. I'll give her a call and she'll come and get me!"

"Oh—okay. Yu call har yet?"

Frustration was building as he said, "No, I haven't!"

"Well, wey yu a lef so early if yu nah call har yet?"

"Ms. Mellie! Why are you asking so many questions? Just get off my back! Devin was angry now and his old nasty ways were churning and spilling over on Mellie.

Not moved by the tone of his angry voice, Mellie said, "Misa Devin, wey yu no sid down and eat?"

Yelling, he said, "Ms. Mellie, please! I told you I'm not hungry!" Devin could no longer take her prodding and questioning; he could not contain his emotion.

"Aright, Misa Devin, aright." Mellie turned around and mumbled as she walked away.

"Ms. Mellie!"

Mellie stopped in her tracks. Turning to face him, you could now see that Mellie was upset as she walked back over to Devin. Placing her hands on her hips, she said, "Misa Devin, I know yu goin tru a lot right now, but if yu goin continue to yell and raise yah voice pon me, mi nah go allow dat. Yu really doan know me, cuz if yu did, yu dat know it a tek a lot for me to stand here and let yu do what yu jus do by talkin de way yu did to me. Mi doan usually let dat happen, but dis marnin durin mi prayar time. Gad tell mi dat I wudda hav di confrontation wid yu and dat mi wuz to let yu have yu sey. Therefore, mi a go be obedien to mi Fadda Gad and let yu get all of yu frustration out. Now sid down and let me get yu sum breakfus."

"But—"

With a slightly raised voice, she said, "Sid down, Misa Devin! Sid down now!"

Devin had never been in contact with a woman like Mellie. He was always the one that had control—no one could ever tell him what to do, but this time, Mellie was in control. Submissively, he sat down at the table. He bowed his head as every emotion within him had built up and was now overflowing as tears of anger fell upon the round, oak table. Mellie knew that Devin needed a little time with no comforting—time alone to get all of the anger and frustration from years of rejection he had held onto and used to abuse others. She made the excuse of getting his food and walked away singing, "Have thine own way Lawd, have thine own way...Yu are de potta, I am de clay."

# CHAPTER 29
## Trevor's Mission

The next day, Trevor drove to his office and could not help but think about Rachel's suffering at the hands of her brother Devin. Anger once again stirred within his heart against him. Holding tightly to the steering wheel, his knuckles turned white as if he were holding onto Devin's neck, trying to strangle the life out of him. He had to remind himself of the scripture that says, "Be angry and sin not."

Over and over he questioned in his mind, how Devin could do such a thing? How can I make him pay for what he did to Rachel? He destroyed her childhood and maturity as a woman. I'm going to make him pay for every night, every minute, every hour she had to endure the pain and suffering of his abuse. Trevor could not fathom how this demonic person could have taken hold and ravaged her youthful, innocent life the way he did. It hurt him to see her cry and the pain that he saw in her eyes was hard to erase from his analytical mind. Shaking his head, he said, "I can't let that coward get away with this—his own sister?"

Pushing the OnStar button, he made a call to Vincent Colbridge, a close friend at the District Attorney's office, but got his voicemail forcing Trevor to leave a message.

"Hey, Vinnie—this is Trevor Danison. Please give me a call as soon as possible. I need your advice about something…got a few questions for you. Call me at the office; I'll be there most of the day. Hope I can talk to you sooner, rather than later."

Ending his call, Trevor mumbled, "I'll take care of this, Rachel—I got you, babe."

He tried to control the anger that rushed through his veins like hot oil. This was now personal. As a detective with the police department, too many of these cases had crossed his desk more times than he wanted to count or even think about. The outcomes were never a pretty picture. Lives had been destroyed at the hands of pathetic, sex-driven men and he was tired of it. This one was close to him now and he wanted to deal with it expeditiously. Devin had crossed the line and would pay a heavy penalty, but not by Trevor's hands—he would put it in the hands of the law.

# CHAPTER 30

## Michael Makes Amends

Michael sat in his office feeling a little better after his night of drinking and revelation. He knew in his heart that either he had to change or the situation had to change and that no matter what, he would have to be the catalyst for whatever change took place. Picking up the phone, he dialed and waited.

"This is Jessie."

"Hi, Jess."

"Hey — what's up, boss?"

"Are you back in town?"

"I'm back."

"How was it traveling with your mom?'

"Pretty good. We got to talk about a lot of things, especially family issues. I learned some interesting things from her...kind of enjoyed it."

"That's good. Hey, listen, I've got a job for you. Come to the mansion. No, wait. Instead, meet me at the restaurant...30...40 minutes?"

"In 30 minutes...okay...gotcha."

Hanging up the phone, Michael went right over to his wall safe that was hidden behind an electronic paneled piece in the wall. He pulled out the box of jewelry he had stolen from Rachel. The box itself looked and felt pretty expensive. It was a red velvet box with a gold, hand-painted design of a floral pattern on top, and gold gimp braid trim framing the bottom. When he opened the box, sadness filled his heart as he looked at the jewelry and thought about what it took to get it. Too many people were involved in his plot, putting lives in major danger. Although he wasn't there when it happened, he was just as guilty since it was the cause of an accidental death— Rachel's Aunt Myra. All he could do was hope and pray that no one would ever find out what he had done. Things had to change and he was about to set it in motion by first returning the jewelry with Jess's help.

***

Before he got to the office, Michael's first stop was the Post Office where he purchased a brown corrugated box. Carefully wrapping the jewelry box in bubble wrap, he then placed it inside the brown box, making sure it was safe and would not be damaged during its return home.

At the restaurant, Michael's staff readied for the dinner crowd. Things were a little quiet at the moment, so when he got there he went straight into his office, placed the box on his desk and waited for Jess to arrive.

Sitting down in his cushy, black leather chair, he began to look through bills that had piled up on his desk and began writing checks to his vendors. One of the things that Michael had failed to do was hire a new secretary. Jennifer, his former secretary, quit due to death in her family and sickness. Revenge against Devin and hard heartedness had gotten in the way of his taking care of business. Now bills for the restaurant were backed up—he wondered how things could still be running as smoothly as they seemed to be.

There was a knock at his office door.

"Come in."

"Hey, boss."

"Jess—thanks for getting here so quickly."

"What's up, boss?"

"Have a seat. You remember the jewelry we heisted from Devin Vandelyn?"

"Yeah...what about it?"

"Well, believe it or not, I want to return it to his sister, Rachel."

Confusion crossed Jess's face as he said, "You're kidding me—right?"

"No, Jess...I'm not."

"But why?" he asked, shaking his head and hunching his shoulders up. "What's up with this?"

Michael sighed deeply and said hesitantly, "My sister."

"Your sister? I'm sorry, boss, but I am totally confused. What in the heck do you mean?"

"Remember those diaries I got when she died?"

"Yeah."

"Well, I've been reading them."

"No! Are you serious? That's kinda personal—isn't it?"

"Yes, but I needed to do it. It's been refreshing and I've learned a lot about Melinda, what she went through and her experiences."

"Hmm...So what's that got to do with returning the jewelry? That stuff is worth a lot of dough."

"Melinda met Rachel."

"Yeah? And?"

"And she liked her. Rachel actually tried to help Melinda and even tried to warn her about Devin. She was nice to my baby sis so I can't see myself continuing to do this to her. She meant a lot to my Melinda. Rachel is not my problem...it's Devin. I have to give this jewelry back to her, right away."

"Boss, excuse me, but right now you're sounding like a man off his rocker."

"Jess...I'm not—I'm being very sensible and I am in my right mind. Just do it!"

"What do you mean, just do it? Boss, I'm not about to get caught and end up in jail because you can't make up your mind, going back and forth on this issue. Either you want revenge or you don't."

"Jess, I'll have my revenge, but I can no longer involve Rachel. Put this box on her doorstep, leave it there and sit back in your car. Watch and make sure that either she or that other girl are the only ones who pick it up. You got me?"

Jess looked at Michael in utter disbelief, but knew that when Michael Stern wanted something, you had to do it. His subtlety was a trait you didn't want to mess with. So Jess agreed and said, "I got you, boss...I'll do it."

He picked up the box, stood up and as he was walking out of the office, Michael said, "Jess...wait!"

"Change your mind, boss?"

"No...here's a bonus check for your work this week."

"Thanks, boss." Jess took the check while shaking his head, and walked out to take care of business.

# CHAPTER 31
## Anita Returns Home

Rachel couldn't help but think about her night with Trevor and how she finally broke down and confided in him about her past. This really saddened her because she let it disrupt what should have been an enjoyable evening with a friend. It also should have been a time to get answers about who Michael Stern was. That day on the nature trail still haunted her, knowing that she allowed herself to be caught in a dangerous situation and was no closer to getting an answer. Rachel didn't feel safe even leaving her home.

The only bright light in this whole scenario was that Trevor stopped by before going to work that morning and promised to keep checking in on her. Tears glistened in her eyes as his voice resonated within her saying, *Rachel, my love, don't let your past dictate our future. I love you and nothing that Devin or anyone else has done in your past is going to change what I'm feeling about you right now.* Cupping her head in the palms of his hands, they kissed and he reiterated his unconditional love for her. This time, her tears were not from hurt, but from an inability to fathom how someone could still love her, knowing the shame she allowed to happen and had to endure for so many years.

Angry at herself, her echo filled the room when she yelled, as if trying to reprimand herself, "Why didn't I stop Devin sooner?...Why, God?...Why?" Not expecting an instant answer, she plopped down on the staircase. Time stood still as an inner peace and calmness suddenly overtook her and a whispering voice within said, *Rachel, when you are weak, I am made strong. Lessons are learned in times of trial. Now, you have a new aim in life – to enjoy it. Don't dwell on your bitter past...It's time to press forward and I will do a new work in you.* At first it caught her off guard, but then she thought about the choices she had: either continue to live a sad and less meaningful life, or choose to be happy and pursue her dreams. She chose the latter telling herself, *Yes, Lord, it's time to stop with my pity parties.*

Rachel stood up, wiped away her tears and forced herself to dance to music that she alone could hear as a symphony played in her head. It was a happy song of freedom and deliverance. A smile appeared as she wrapped her arms around her thin frame thinking about what was to come. There was now a new-found determination to bury the past and move on to a greater future with a man who loved her despite all she had done and been through.

Her dancing happily suddenly stopped when she heard keys jingling in the keyhole. The only person with access to her home was Anita. All the locks had been changed when she found out that even after Aunt Myra took the keys from Devin, he somehow made duplicates. Rachel knew Anita would be returning from her family reunion but still, nervousness welled up within her as she dreaded not knowing who would be entering into her home.

She began to think, *Where can I hide? What if it's not Anita?* Turning to find a place of escape, she stopped in her tracks when Anita came in struggling to hold on to two pieces of luggage, and a square brown box tightly tucked under her left arm. Anita also kicked another piece of luggage into the hallway.

"Anita!" There was an air of excitement as Rachel ran over to embrace her friend, causing Anita to drop the two cases she had in her hands, but the box was saved so Anita immediately sat it on a table which held a large, wicker basket.

"I'm so glad you're back!" Rachel said, smiling ear to ear.

"It's so good to be home!" Anita said, hugging her.

"I thought you'd never return. I missed you so much."

"Oh, did you now? Did you miss my taking care of business or my friendship?"

"Both," said Rachel, and they laughed.

Almost tripping over the luggage, Anita caught herself and walked over to the sofa and plopped down.

"Whew…It feels good to finally relax and take a load off my feet. These dogs are barkin' loud." So she kicked off her shoes and began rubbing her toes and said, "Thank you, Jesus!!"

"So…how was the reunion?" asked Rachel.

"Well, even though it was a reunion, it was supposed to at least feel as if I was on vacation. That didn't happen—I worked. You know how it is when you get around family. Things were so unorganized—I ended up being the one handling people and their issues. I also had to make some other major arrangements."

"Well, that wasn't much of a vacation—was it?" Rachel said as she sat down next to her.

"You got that right. I did get to go to the beach on the first day. It was beautiful just sitting there watching the waves of the blue water crash against the cliffs. It felt good to have hot sand easing between my toes. But…that was short lived. My brother, Papo, and his wife thought they had everything together. Rachel, it was a genuine, tailor-made mess. I couldn't believe what I was seeing—I had to take over. I just couldn't stand there and let things go on the way they were. It would have been so embarrassing. Memaw would have been turning over in her grave had I not stepped in and taken over."

Rachel sat there shaking her head and said, "Girl, you are so anal."

"Just like my grandma," she said with a smile.

"No, but look...At the banquet, it looked like they had taken up a donation for the dinnerware from family members. There was a myriad of colored plates...nothing matched. It would have been different if they were at least the same design, but no! They just threw stuff together. Even the tablecloths were a hot mess. Wrinkled plastic—I found a hole in one. They must have been recycled from some other banquet. I put a stop to the madness and we went to the dollar store and picked up some new plates and even got matching napkins and plastic silverware that looked like real silverware. We rented the tablecloths from a restaurant franchise."

"Anita, you took down everything they had prepared?"

"You're darn right I did."

"I'm sure they must have appreciated it though— right?"

Looking upward and rolling her eyes, Anita said, "Well, at first my sister-in-law seemed to have a real attitude with me. But I was cool...I didn't let it bother me. I just said in my intellectual mind, *You just wait and see...just wait.* Rachel, when we put it all together, the turquoise and white looked so pretty. You should have seen her then. Jade was so excited about it because she saw what we were able to accomplish together as a team."

"That's good. I'm glad things turned out the way you wanted."

With that, Anita jumped up and grabbed her smaller piece of luggage. Reaching into it, she pulled out an odd-shaped package that was wrapped securely in newspaper and brown paper.

"Here—this is for you," she said, handing the package to Rachel.

Carefully removing the wrapping, Rachel smiled, saying, "Oh, Anita—this is beautiful." A tall, hand-blown, glass teardrop vase that reflected a carnival of pastel colors was presented to Rachel.

"Anita—I love it. Thank you so much!" Rachel said, hugging her.

"Oh, you're welcome. I saw it in the market square at Horan's and thought it would be something that you'd like since it's so artsy," she proudly said.

Sitting back down on the sofa, Anita leaned over with elbows propped on her knees, and looking down at the floor, she softly said, "Rachel, I have something I need to tell you."

Rachel got up and walked over to the mantel, carefully setting the vase down. Turning to Anita, she said, "Okay—sounds like it's about to get hot and heavy— what's wrong?"

"Nothing's wrong, but I do have something important to say to you." Anita stood up and walked over to Rachel. With head bowed, she took a deep breath and then lifted her head to look Rachel in her eyes.

"Rachel, while I was away, I made a very important decision."

Sensing it was going to be something that she wouldn't like, but wanted to get it said and done with, Rachel said, "Anita, what kind of decision? Please, just…just go ahead and say whatever it is."

Anita felt like she wanted to turn away and change her mind about saying anything. As she stood there, beads of sweat formed on her forehead. All the way back from her trip, she rehearsed in her mind the words she would say and how she would say them. Now it came down to this moment in time and she was still unsure of how she would share her news with Rachel. This was harder than she thought.

Anita took a deep breath and then slowly said, "Well…you know how I've been talking about one day moving back home? I…I've decided that now is the time to do it…I'm going to move back home."

"Home — Bermuda?" Rachel's heart pumped fast as anxiety built up when she thought about the prospect of Anita leaving her for good.

"Yes, Bermuda."

Rachel felt a searing scream waiting to explode from within, but squelched it, trying to hold back, not wanting to make Anita feel bad about her decision. It was a topic that had been in the air for a long time, but Rachel never thought it would be something that would ever come to pass. Her friend had a life to live outside of being a personal assistant, and Rachel didn't want to get in the way of what life had destined for Anita. So she tried hard to hold back the feelings that were raging uncontrollably within.

"When?"

"At the end of next month, if that's okay with you?"

With voice a little raised, she said, "Okay, Anita—anything you want to do is okay with me. You don't have to get *my* permission when it comes to your personal life. I'm happy for you—okay? Of course I'll be sad to see you go—that's just part of being human. I mean—you've been with us for so many years. I always thought that we would be friends for life, here...in this house...not separated by distance."

"I hear what you're saying, Rachel, but I have a feeling that deep inside, you're really having a problem with it."

"Anita...Why wouldn't I have a problem? The problem I'm having is being alone...first without Aunt Myra, now you're leaving me. That's the problem," she said shaking her head.

As hard as she tried, she couldn't control her voice that began quaking and showing emotion. "Anita, you're like family to me and I'd hate to see you go, but life is too precious not to be doing something that makes you happy. So if moving back home does that for you then do it! That's all that really matters."

Calming a bit, she softly said, "You did a lot for my aunt while she was here and there's never been anything in writing that said you had to continue on here with me. I'm a big girl now and I know how to take care of myself. I'm... I'm just disappointed—and will miss you girl," Rachel said, balling her fist and lightly punching Anita in the arm.

"I know—but you'll be fine. While I'm here, though, I'll make sure everything is in order so that you'll have few, if any, problems when I leave. I'll get all of the paperwork together, bank statements and whatever you need so that I can show you exactly what to do. Things will run smoothly and stress free—you'll be okay; I know you will.

Rachel sat down on the sofa and hid her face, trying to hide a single tear that escaped and rolled down her cheek. Quickly whisking the tear away, she softly said, "Yes, I'll be just fine. Time to put my big girl panties on."

Anita smiled and gave her a big hug.

"Okay...that's enough." She got up and walked over to get her luggage.

"Oh Rachel, this box was in the doorway." She handed the brown square box to Rachel.

Satisfied that Rachel received the box just as Michael requested, Jess drove away and made a call informing him that the jewelry had been safely delivered.

# CHAPTER 32

## Rachel is Bemused

The day had been a long and emotional one. When Anita gave her the news about leaving, the day took an unimaginable turn, making her feel a bit of sadness. *How will I survive without my friend? She's been with us for so many years and I'm truly going to miss her,* she thought. In spite of it all, it was a very satisfying, life-changing, thought provoking day for Rachel...something she would not soon forget, and now things were about to get heavier.

Taking the box that Anita found on the doorstep, Rachel went to the privacy of her bedroom to open the mysterious package. Wonderment filled her mind as she slowly removed the wrapping from the cardboard box. She began to surmise. *Who can this be from? There's no return address, but it's addressed to me. I haven't ordered anything online — what can this be?* Removing the bubble wrap, tears filled her eyes as she recognized the red velvet and gold, hand-painted box.

"Aunt Myra — it's Aunt Myra's jewelry box. My God — I've gotten it back!"

For a moment, joy filled her heart. Gratefulness for the returned heirloom was overwhelming until she remembered the circumstances by which she temporarily lost ownership. *What is happening?* she thought. A chill ran through her veins as she recalled Devin's words on the day she handed the jewelry box over to the strange woman. *I need that jewelry or they are going to kill you and me.* These were the words of her brother — a person whom she despised.

Now this same jewelry was back in her shaking hands after being used as a threat to take their lives. "What is going on here? Where is Devin? I've got to talk to him. Anita!!"

Jumping up from her bed, she rushed down the stairs, almost tripping as she headed to the first floor and banged on Anita's door shouting, "Anita! Anita I need to talk with you!"

Anita's shower was disrupted by the cries of Rachel. Quickly jumping from the shower, she wrapped her bathrobe around her wet body and found a frantic Rachel standing outside the door with teary eyes.

"Rachel, what's wrong? What happened? Why are you yelling like this?"

"The jewelry — I've gotten it back! Aunt Myra's jewelry is back!"

"What do you mean, you got it back? It's in a safe at the bank. What's wrong with you, Rachel?"

She had never told Anita about the dangerous situation that Devin had involved them in. Rachel knew what Anita would say and did not want to put her in harm's way.

"Rachel, calm down—calm down. What's this all about?"

As she presented the jewelry box before Anita, Rachel could see the surprise on her face as she said, "No, it wasn't in the safe deposit box. It hasn't been for some time now."

Taking a seat on the couch, Rachel began to explain all that had happened. Anita sat there awestruck. She shook her head in disbelief and became even angrier with each exposed detail of this devious plot that kept danger on their doorstep.

"Rachel, this is totally ridiculous. I'm sorry, but I can't stand your evil brother. We need to call the authorities, this has got to stop! You can't let him get away with this! Enough is enough! First, he rapes your body and then he rapes you of what you have left of your Aunt Myra—a valuable irreplaceable gift to you! I'm calling the police!"

"No, Anita! You can't do that! I don't know why the jewelry was returned or who put it on the doorstep. I'm afraid that whoever it was will come back looking for it! This could be a trick! We need to call Devin and see if he knows anything."

"Are you sure, Rachel? This is some serious mess he's gotten you into. He can't slide by this time—something has got to be done right away."

"Yes, something does have to be done, but not right now. The only person we should be calling is Devin. We need to see what he has to say about this first and then we can go from there."

"But, Rachel!"

"No, Anita…It has to be done this way for right now. Please bear with me."

"Okay…okay—I guess so," said Anita reluctantly. "I'll get us a cup of chamomile tea so we can settle down and then I'll try and figure out where the devil boy is."

"Thanks, Anita."

# CHAPTER 33
## Devin's Redemption

Although it was a short span of time that Devin spent with Jeremiah and Ms. Mellie, he felt something deep within beginning to change—things were not the same. There was an air of positivism flowing in his heart and mind. Not knowing how he originally ended up at The Arc was still a major mystery that consumed him mentally. Jeremiah persisted in trying to convince the doubting Devin that it was the power of God that brought him there. Having no real belief in God and in what He was able to do was proving to be a real hindrance for Devin. At times he would fight back, questioning the authenticity of statements made about this deity called God.

There were times when certain things started to make a little sense, but Devin would not easily concede. He always insisted on more proof. One time he said, "Show me in some tangible way that what you're saying is true—it's just hard to believe that there's a God who can really love me the way I am."

No longer wanting to come off as being sarcastic and callous, Devin finally decided that he would stop and listen carefully as Jeremiah took time to explain the words he read from the Bible. His heart was no longer hardened and he wanted to learn more and stop rejecting what was being said. At first the Bible seemed like a strange book to Devin but, as time went on, he began accepting it and became engrossed in what he read within the lines and text of the scriptures.

A few times he found himself somewhat emotional—holding back tears that rested in the corner of his tired eyes. To hide his feelings, he would jump up and pace the floor and then turn his back on Jeremiah, quickly wiping away any tears that ran down his face.

Something was happening and Devin was in denial of any feelings. As he sat in his room on the last night of his stay, he thought about the weekend, all he had been through, done and heard during his sessions with Jeremiah. He was guilt ridden with thoughts of the past that pressured his mind.

He tried getting a good night of rest but a battle between good and evil ensued. Emotionally drained, he struggled to make sense of it all. He dropped to his knees weeping profusely and began to pray. All night long, warfare erupted in his mind. He dreamt of the demons that had possessed him throughout most of his life, wrapping chains around his neck and pulling him into a deep, heated pit. As they struggled to pull him into this pit, he heard the voice of Rachel screaming for him to get off of her and his Aunt Myra calling him a thief. His sanity was on the line as he fought viciously to prevent the demons from taking total control. This was a battle that he wanted to win—it was his time to be free. He was tired of the life he was living and was no longer willing to be consumed with a life filled with hate and deceit. He wanted a good life—a life of love that would be fulfilling in the way it should have been from the beginning. He no longer wanted to be viewed as if he was a demon, but he wanted a true, non-judgmental relationship with new friends...especially his family.

At mid-morning he fell asleep in a corner that became an altar of prayer on the hardwood floor. He was now at peace as he lay comfortably in that spot—sleeping until late in the day.

A heavy-handed knock on the door was his wake up call.

"Devin—Misa Devin, yu wake? Misa Devin!"

He pried his eyes open that were encrusted due to the salty tears of a long, bitter night, and said, "Yes—yes—Ms. Mellie."

"Can I cum in?"

"Just one minute."

Rubbing his eyes to get the sleep out, Devin slowly got up from the floor. Getting up was a challenge; every bone in his body was stiff. He felt as if he had just been through boot camp with a herd of large buffalo running through an elevated rocky plain.

"Mmm, man! Why am I so sore?" Devin said as he rubbed his left shoulder and grabbed his robe making his way to the door. The pleasant aroma of food wafted through the air. Opening the door, Ms. Mellie stood there with a large platter of delicious-looking cuisine. Red beans and rice with stewed chicken, cabbage, and two buttermilk biscuits with a side of honey tantalized his voracious taste buds.

Smiling she said, "Misa Devin—me tink you wuz ded de way yu wuz sleepin dis marning. Yu hungry? Me bring yu a plate of food."

"Thanks, Ms. Mellie."

Entering the room, Mellie set the platter on an empty table and said, "Misa, Devin—call me Mellie. Yu a my frien and yu can call me Mellie now."

Those words meant so much to Devin. It had been a long road for the two of them and he appreciated the fact that things had changed so much that she would allow him to call her Mellie. Not too many people were given the right to call this fireball of a woman by her first name. It was something that, in Mellie's eyes, had to be earned.

"I can? Are you sure? No more Ms. Mellie?"

"Yes, sir, me sure," she proudly said.

"Thanks, Mellie."

Before he sat to eat, Devin ran into the bathroom, brushed his teeth and washed his face. Looking into the mirror, he thought about his restless night and the struggle he fought for control. He won. Devin could not help but admit, surely, there must be a God. A new found peace filled his heart and he could not wait to share what he felt with his family.

Sitting down with Mellie was a pleasure this time. She was his new friend and he enjoyed her company. Hearing stories of her homeland was an education in itself. He would never forget this moment in time as he sat with her in fellowship—the two of them talking as he enjoyed the savory flavors of her phenomenal cooking. Devin was a changed man.

# CHAPTER 34

## Trevor Faces the Enemy

"Rachel, I've been trying to contact Devin but his phone goes straight to voicemail."

"It must need charging. How could he let it die like that?" she said, shaking her head in frustration.

"Anita, I really need to find out where he is. As strange as it may seem, I'm a little concerned about not being able to contact him."

"Why, Rachel? Devin has meant nothing but trouble for you."

"But, I haven't heard anything from him in a few days. What if it has something to do with me getting Aunt Myra's jewelry back? He was so desperate for me to get it from the safe deposit because of the death threats, and wanted to make sure that the person who was threatening us was satisfied and would not make good on those threats."

"Rachel, how do you know that all of this is not just a trick...a scam on his part? He's such a deceitful person.

He could have been perpetrating a fraud to get the jewelry. It's worth over $40,000 and he most likely knows that."

"Anita, I thought the same thing until he took off his shirt and showed me his beaten and bruised body. He was beaten so badly by these people—contusions were all over his chest and especially in his stomach and back. I thought all of this was settled—I'm scared and my mind is thinking all kinds of crazy things. Where is he? Where is Devin?"

"Rachel, are you sure you don't want me to call the police about this?"

"I'm sure, Anita."

"Okay—so if not the police, what about Detective Danison? What if I call him? He'd know what to do in this situation. Rachel, please? This is serious."

Taking a deep breath, she knew that something had to be done—was this the time? Rachel was hesitant in calling Trevor since she had already confided in him about how Devin had sexually molested her. How would he handle this on top of what he had just learned about Devin?

"I don't know, Anita—I just don't know if I want to bring him into this."

"Rachel! I'm in this house and you're putting my life in danger too! I can't see myself sitting back not knowing what's going to happen next. I can't let you do this to us. I'll be leaving you soon and I don't want the job of worrying about our safety my last days here. Now you can either let me call Detective Danison or I'm calling the police — it's your choice!"

Seeing Anita's desperate concern, Rachel conceded and said, "Okay, call Trevor."

He wasted no time coming over. Walking through the door, Trevor embraced Rachel and passionately kissed her.

Anita smiled, saying, "Wow — what just happened? What is this intimacy I'm seeing? What happened while I was away?"

Rachel smiled and held onto Trevor's hand as they walked into the living room.

"Okay, ladies — what's going on here? What's this big emergency?" Trevor said as they sat down.

Rachel explained everything that had happened after her Aunt Myra's death and how Devin had convinced her that there was a death threat — one that had even caused the accidental death of her aunt.

"So that's why you were so suspicious when you called me in to investigate her death. Now I see why," said Trevor.

Rachel emphatically said, "No, Trevor...all of this happened afterwards. As a matter of fact, it was the day of our first date."

He shook his head, stood and said, "Rachel, I'm so tired of hearing how your brother continually causes so much hurt in your life and gets away with it. Something has got to be done—I'm not going to let him continue to hurt you like this—it just can't happen anymore!"

"I told her the same thing, Detective."

Hearing the door close, they all stopped and looked. Devin stood there with a smile on his face.

"Hey! Are you folks talking about me? The door was unlocked. I let myself in."

Shocked to see him standing there, Rachel stood and almost ran toward him, but stopped herself, remembering who he had been in her life. Anger overtook her as she yelled, "Where have you been!"

Trevor looked at Devin with burning anger in his heart and a strong desire to assault him saying, "Well...well...this must be the infamous Devin Vandelyn that I've heard so much about."

Surprised by his bitter hostility, Devin sarcastically said, "Yes, that's who I am—the infamous, Devin Vandelyn here in the flesh."

Rachel tried to stop Trevor, but failed to intervene as he rushed to Devin and stood face to face with him.

With red hot anger seething through his blood, Trevor stood with a balled up fist at his side wanting to plummet Devin. He contained his anger and said, "I've heard too much about you and what you've done to your sister. You should be buried in the very pit of hell for all you've done, you nasty little prick. What is it with you that you can take advantage of your own sister, steal from your aunt, cause her death and then let your drunken, low-down self cause death threats to be placed upon this family? Well, you know what? You've done your last bit of dirt! You won't get away with anything else, if it's the last thing I do. I'm going to see your perverted tail in somebody's prison."

Devin just stood there, feeling the heat of Trevor's breath along his face and a convicting sting within his heart. In the past, angry words spoken against him had no effect—this time they did. Knowing the weightiness of the situation, he didn't say a word; he silently stood there and listened. When Trevor finished degrading him, Devin reached into his back pocket, pulling out his cell phone and presented it to Trevor saying, "Here—make the call. I'm everything you said and deserve to serve my time and more."

Knocking the phone to the floor, Trevor yelled, "I don't need your phone...I've got my own, thank you—I have the number of a good friend in the District Attorney's office. We've already been discussing you and have had more than enough of our share of maniacs like you."

Devin looked over at Rachel and said, "Sis, I'm sincerely sorry for all the pain and suffering I caused you and the family. I don't know what I can do or say that will make you ever believe me when I say that I am a changed man—I'm being truthful and sincere about this."

As he spoke, a tear trickled down the side of his face. Rachel and Anita both stood there in silence—stunned at what they were seeing. This was the first time that they'd ever seen an emotional side of Devin.

"Trevor—wait!" Rachel shouted as she pulled on his arm.

"Rachel, you can't let him continue to do these things to you."

"I know, but—"

"Don't let this guy fool you into believing anything. He's been deceitful most of his life...he'll never change," said Trevor angrily.

"But, Trevor, he's my brother. Besides, I need to hear what he has to say about this jewelry. Why was it returned?"

Surprise filled Devin's face as he inquired, "What are you talking about, Rachel? What jewelry?"

"Stop playing stupid, Devin. What do you know about Aunt Myra's jewelry being returned to me? It was on the doorstep wrapped in a brown cardboard box."

Reaching for it, he said, "There must be some mistake—it can't be Aunt Myra's jewelry. Let me see it."

Rachel handed the jewelry box to Devin and watched him carefully as he opened the box.

His eyes were filled with disbelief as he examined the jewelry. With a raised voice he said, "This can't be." Shaking his head, he handed the jewelry box back to Rachel and said, "Honestly, I don't know anything about this. I really don't know what to say and how to deal with it. I didn't have anything to do with this, Rachel."

Trevor walked away, sat on the sofa and said, "Well, I don't believe you. You've been lying and cheating your way through life, so why should anyone believe you now? Just come clean, Devin. Your sister's life is in jeopardy."

"Come on—I swear I don't know anything about this. I'm just as puzzled as you are. How can I make you understand that I'm not lying? I don't know a thing!"

Rachel sat down next to Trevor and asked him, "What should we do now?"

"Do you believe him, Rachel? Do you really believe what this guy is saying?"

Hesitating, Rachel glared at Devin and then looked at Trevor and said, "Yes, Trevor—I do—I believe him."

"You're sure about this?"

Rachel looked over at Devin and then again at Trevor. Taking a deep breath, she shook her head saying, "Yes."

Giving in, Trevor said, "Okay, babe, but we need to first think about this."

There was an awkward silence as Devin walked over to the other side of the room, isolated from everyone else to sit down on a black, leather ottoman.

Trevor got up from the sofa and stood before the three of them as if he were a lawyer in court, giving a summation in a crowded courtroom. Rubbing his chin, he said, "Alright, then...first thing we must do is take him down to the police station and get a statement. Then we'll see if we can get an investigation underway. If there's danger involved, we need to see who we're dealing with. Whoever took the jewelry is either giving up or is playing a game of deception and will be back for it."

He went and sat down next to Rachel. She wrapped her arms around his waist, laying her head on his chest as he sat back on the couch.

"Rachel, I really need you to know that I'm going to get to the bottom of this. No one will ever hurt you again," he said with eyes locked on Devin. "I'll never let that happen again…never!"

# CHAPTER 35

## Devin is Made Accountable

D ays passed and things were quiet. Nothing was heard from Michael Stern regarding the jewelry. A report was placed with the police department and, for now, Devin was free on his own recognizance. Trevor was given a key to the house and he was in and out, making sure that Rachel and Anita were safe.

Devin kept in constant contact with Jeremiah and Mellie; it helped to keep him grounded with his new life in a positive way. Things also changed in his relationship with Rachel. Slowly, but surely, they were able to cope with each other, even holding decent conversations with the ability to be in each other's company for a greater length of time.

Devin had learned lessons from Jeremiah that were kept at the forefront of his mind. One thing, in particular, that Jeremiah said stuck with Devin daily: Learn from your past as you take time each day to see how you can become a vehicle for good and not for evil.

In honor of seeking to live a better life, he started going to church and volunteered his services in the youth department. Known as Mr. D by the young fatherless boys, he began by mentoring and tutoring them in the Kingdom Movers' program.

While Devin was doing his best to change his life, Michael Stern was making plans of his own to make it miserable. He had not given up on his quest and hated Devin even more as he continued reading journal after journal. Learning a lot from his sister, he decided on a different tactic when it came to getting his revenge. Hiring the best attorney in the city, Michael decided to see how he could bring Devin's accountability into question in the death of his sister.

There was one journal entry that he could not shake as his vendetta grew more intense against Devin.

> "Dear Mr. Diary,
>
> Today I am filled with hatred toward him. I called to find out why he would cause so much disgrace by leaving me standing at the altar. He said that he never loved me...he said he was marrying me just because I got pregnant! Yes — I messed up and I got pregnant! But I lost the baby — I lost my baby."

As Michael read, he cried and became even more upset at seeing what looked like teardrops on the tattered, yellow page. After drying his tears, he continued to read.

"It was Devin's fault — his entire fault that I lost the baby. It was so stressful once we set the date for the wedding — especially the week before the ceremony. That was a day that I will never, ever forget. I went to his apartment and he'd been drinking — again. Things were a mess. Empty alcohol bottles were all over the place and in trying to clean up I found a pair of semen smeared women's bikini panties that did not belong to me. I questioned him about it, but he denied everything saying that they belonged to me. I don't wear bikinis — they just don't fit right on me. But he continually denied it. He yelled and told me to leave. He actually pushed me out the door, quickly closing it behind me. I was so angry.

Burning tears blinded my eyes as I hurried to get away from the pain he had caused. Not seeing clearly, I tripped and fell down a short flight of stairs. That night I started bleeding and had to go to the hospital. There was nothing that could be done; I had lost the baby. Even in trying to console me, he seemed quite happy that it happened. Things were not the same between us after that. I guess this was his way out of marrying me.

The night before the wedding, I had a feeling that our wedding day would be a disaster. I jokingly said, 'Devin, if you don't show up for the wedding, I'll just want to die.' His cold response was, 'Go ahead and die'. I laughed it off, *but inside it hurt so bad to hear those words spew from his mouth. I knew he wasn't playing, but I was in denial of his real love for me. So he did it...left me...didn't show up for the wedding. Now, this life really has no more meaning for me — I can't breathe without him. I'm sorry, Michael."*

Those were the last words written in her journal...words that screamed loud and were deafening to Michael when he realized that it was the end of her journey in this life. Melinda lost it emotionally and it was on that night when she took her life dressed in her Vera Wang custom-made wedding gown in a carbon monoxide-filled garage. Pictures of better days with Devin surrounded Melinda in the red PT Cruiser that Michael had especially customized for her.

He was now out for total revenge. More tears rolled down his face as he looked upon this final, brown-stained page that was filled with her dried tears. Michael seethed inside, almost tearing his fingernails off as they dug deep into the old wooden table where he sat weeping while reading about the hurt and pain his baby sister had endured her last days. There were no words to describe how he was feeling at that moment. There was nothing that could change his mind about Devin's responsibility in her death. If the law couldn't take care of this, he would do it. Devin had to pay! Devin Vandelyn, you've been served.

# CHAPTER 36

## Devin is Served

A t day's end, Devin settled down on his twill sofa in an effort to ease his wearied body. In his hand he held his favorite coffee mug. In times past that mug would be filled with his friend, vodka. But on this night, it was filled with earl gray tea, made with two tea bags and honey. It was his new addiction. Swallowing it down to the last drop, he dozed off with the warm cup still in his hand. Tiredness caused him to sleep through the night on the usually uncomfortable sofa. An early morning bang on the door jolted him out of deep sleep, causing Devin to drop the empty mug onto the floor. Quickly sitting up, he rubbed his eyes and groggily shouted, "Just a minute! Hold on!"

He got up and tried to get his balance. For a moment, Devin stood there making the impatient intruder wait while he stretched, creating a loud growling sound as he yawned. Picking his mug up from the floor, he sat it on a nearby table. As he walked toward the door, another heavy-handed bang was discharged, almost knocking down a picture that hung on the wall adjacent to the door.

"Geesh!! Who is it!! Stop banging—give me a break!"

When he opened the door, a man dressed in a dark gray uniform stood before him and said, "Are you Mr. Devin Vandelyn?"

"Yes, I am. And who are you? Why are you banging like a madman on my door at this time of morning?"

"This is for you, Mr. Vandelyn—you've been served."

"What is this? Hey! What is this?"

Without explanation, the courier turned and walked away. As Devin opened the envelope, he could not believe what he was reading. His past had now caught up with him and Melinda was reaching for him from the grave getting her revenge. A cold chill made its way through his body as he read the charges and saw that he would have to appear before a judge.

"What is this? She committed suicide! My fault? No! I didn't have any—"

His ranting stuck in the back of his throat and stopped him cold when he thought about some of the comments he made that could have sent Melinda to her death. He felt an even greater chill creep through his bones that made him quiver uncontrollably.

"No...n-no...It just can't be—I really may have caused her death."

Feeling light-headed, Devin sat at his dining room table and laid the paper document down in front of him. Overcome with grief and the thought of what he had done, he banged his fist on the table and shouted, "Oh my God! What did I do? Oh dear God! Ohhhhh!"

Tears began to flow as he thought about the person he used to be and the hurt he had caused in the life of someone who really loved him.

"I was so evil...and — and...Melinda! I'm so sorry for what I did to you!" Emotions were in full gear as he laid his head on the table and cried.

The ramifications of what he had done became crystal clear in his mind as he pondered every detail of their relationship. Losing the baby from falling down the stairs, telling her to go ahead and die, as well as leaving her at the church altar flooded his now tormented mind. It was a full circle moment for Devin as he read the subpoena that lay before him. It was demanding that he appear to answer questions. He knew that any questions asked would bring back charred memories which had been hidden in the secret places of his mind. Now, he would have to face those demons that he tried so hard to bury from his past as he thought of not only Melinda, but also Rachel and his Aunt Myra — he had devastated their lives.

Anger and hatred swelled up within him as he thought about who he was. He began to question the meaning of his life...what was it worth? What had he really accomplished by hurting others? When he hurt them, he was really hurting himself. This was so real within him that he could no longer put up with himself. Hatred flowed through his veins like a roaring river.

A bottle of vodka sat in one corner of his bookshelf being used as a bookend. Staring intensely at the clear, glass bottle, his mind traveled back to the day Melinda fell down the flight of stairs at his old apartment and lost the baby — his baby. Self-hatred covered his heart. He walked over to the bookshelf and grabbed the bottle of vodka. As he opened the bottle, he drew it close to his nose and took a whiff of the strong aroma that was emitted. Angry, he took the opened bottle and threw it against the wall.

Picking up a jagged piece of the broken glass, he contemplated cutting his wrists. He took a good look at the glass that he held between his thumb and index finger, and said, "No one will ever care if I'm gone — they won't even miss me. I've been so evil, I can't even stand myself. The things I did to her…our baby. I was supposed to be a father! I'm nothing! My life isn't worth living! Why should I even bother going to court and try to make lame excuses for all I did to her?"

Death seemed to be the only way out of his miserable memories — or so he thought. He lifted the jagged glass and looked through it, letting the sunlight of the new day shine through the sharp piece. Bringing it down, he took the glass and placed it onto the skin of his right wrist and then let it rest directly in the center. Feeling a sharp pain, he saw a small drop of blood ooze its way out of his wrist. Tears began to flow as he slumped down with his back against the wall. Realizing that this was not the answer to his problems, he threw the jagged glass down and cried out, "I'm sorry! I'm so sorry, God—please forgive me—Melinda, please forgive me!" His body seized with emotion as he cried out in sorrowful anguish.

Devin sat in that spot for several hours trying to fathom his culpability. Finally picking himself up from the floor, he walked over to the table and, once again, took the subpoena into his trembling hands and began to read the list of charges. Shaking his head, he said, "I will not contest—I'll pay the price for my sins. I deserve severe judgment."

Resolved in what he had to do, he stood up, went to the bathroom to wash his face and then made a call to Jeremiah.

# CHAPTER 37
## The Apology

After speaking with Jeremiah, Devin was much calmer. He knew what had to be done and was all set to do so. His past had finally caught up with him. He confessed his folly and scandalous past to Jeremiah—it was a past that had haunted him for years and seemed to never end. Now, he felt great relief and a sense of freedom. Although he felt better about how things were now evolving, Devin would not be able to move on until he did something more. He had to make peace with his sister, Rachel. He wasn't sure how he would be able to accomplish that, but he was determined to try. Once it was done, the last bit of his life's trial would be to complete the requirements of his court summons. He was not sure what the outcome of the case would be but, with a good lawyer, he was ready to answer any questions and perform any judgments that would apply.

As he drove to Rachel's home, he thought about the nights that he forced himself upon her small frame to satisfy his sexual desires when she was just a child. Guilt ridden, he almost gagged at the thought of all he had done. He knew how hard it would be to make things right—he could not change the past. His greatest hope was that she would accept his apology and be willing to forgive him for every transgression.

Rachel held the keys to his future in her hands. After hearing of his summons, would she also be a witness against him in this same case, revealing the rape and degradation he had perpetrated upon her? This began to weigh heavily on his mind—how would it end? Would she be the one who would seal his fate? He would know soon.

He pulled up into the paved, private driveway and slowly made the turn into the narrow cul-de-sac. At that moment, Devin, who had not yet proclaimed to be a Christian or had conceded in any belief of the existence of God, began to pray. He parked the car and made his way up the concrete walkway. Stopping before he climbed the stairs, Devin tried to gather his thoughts as to what he would say and how to say it. How would he be able to show her real sincerity in his plea so that she'd know how serious he was? This would be the hardest thing he had ever done. He rang the doorbell.

"Who is it?" Rachel shouted from inside the house.

"It's Devin. Let me in, sis."

Hesitating to open the door completely, she stood there eyeing him as if she were trying to decide whether or not to welcome him in. She finally said, "Watch your step—I just washed the floor—it's almost dry. I didn't expect any company today."

"Why are you cleaning? I thought you had a person who did all of that for you."

"I had to get rid of her. I wasn't feeling safe ever since we got the jewelry back. I'm not sure who I can trust now."

"Well, where's Anita?"

"Why are you asking so many questions, Devin? She's gone…back to Bermuda."

"She just got back from visiting there not too long ago. When is she coming back?"

"She's not."

"What do you mean, she's not?"

"It's just what I said—she went back home to live."

"Oh. So you're here—alone? No Trevor?"

"He'll be here soon. Why are you here, Devin? And why are you asking so many questions? My life is none of your concern. You caused enough dilemmas—it still hurts to even think about it."

Rachel reached down and picked up the mail that sat in a bin next to the hall closet. Sitting on the stairs of the spiral staircase, she put on her reading glasses and began flipping through each piece of mail.

"Can we go into the den and talk?" Devin asked.

Suspiciously looking at him over the top of her glasses, she laid the mail down and said, "Let's go in the kitchen. I just put dinner on and don't want it to burn."

Devin nervously followed Rachel into the kitchen with adjudication on his mind.

He sat down at the table while Rachel walked over to the stove and removed the top from a large stock pot and began stirring. He watched as steam escaped, wafting through the air with a delicious aroma.

"What's for dinner?" he asked with a grin.

"Chicken and noodles—It's Aunt Myra's special recipe. Trevor loves it." Placing the top back onto the pot, Rachel asked, "What did you want to talk about, Devin?"

A nervous twinge rose up in his stomach and beads of sweat began to appear on his forehead. Removing a napkin from the holder, Devin took a deep breath and wiped his sweat away.

"Devin, what is it? You seem so nervous and antsy about something. What is it?"

Getting up from the table, Devin walked over to her and with tears welling in his eyes, he said, "Rachel—I want to apologize to you and beg for your pardon."

"What is this, Devin?" Rachel said with anger, backing away from him as if she was now afraid that his old ways were reappearing.

"I'm so sorry for everything that I ever did to you. I regret the times I caused you to suffer under the weight of my body as I raped you for my pleasure, taking advantage of and hurting you."

"Devin!" Rachel screamed as she reached for a steak knife that stood in a bamboo block on the granite countertop. Her hand rested on the wide, stainless steel handle.

"No, Rachel! You don't need that! I'm not trying to hurt you, nor do I want to. I'll never, ever touch you inappropriately again. I have to say something...if I don't say it, I'll never have any real peace. Please listen to me and don't be afraid of me or what I have to say...please, Rachel."

She slowly removed her hand from the knife and stood there, eyes glistening with tears.

"Sis, I was a devilish, demonic fool. I can't tell you how much I hate myself for what I did to you. I know I can never take back the years that I put you through such anguish and pain. I only hope and pray that you will find a little place in your heart to forgive me. My life has taken a major turn—for the better and, Rachel, I am not the same. I can't even begin to explain it, but I am not the same man as I was a few months ago. I am filled with so much self-hatred for what I did to you. If I could, I'd take back every moment of that time and turn it all around to change that evil into good."

As he spoke, Rachel turned away from him as if in disgust.

"Rachel, please look at me — please — I'm begging you to please give me a chance to acknowledge my sins and forgive me. I've never been more serious about anything in my life."

Speechless, she slowly turned and faced Devin with tears flowing down her pained face. Walking toward him, she rushed at him and began punching and plummeting him with all of her might in his chest as she screamed, "I hate you...I hate you, Devin! You ruined my life. You've hurt me so much. You're my brother. You were supposed to protect me and take care of me — not hurt me! Oh, God! Why? Why did you let it happen? Why?"

Devin said nothing. Standing there and taking his beating, he knew that she had every right, so he stood there and took the flailing that he most certainly deserved. Succumbing to exhaustion, Rachel fell into him and Devin embraced her — they both cried.

There was a breakthrough for each of them as Rachel finally released the anger she was feeling toward her brother and laid her head upon his chest. Sobbing, she softly said, "I forgive you — Devin, I forgive you."

Trevor had quietly walked in during Rachel's confrontation with Devin. When he heard what Devin was saying and saw Rachel's reaction, his first inclination was to rush to her aid, but decided that this was a good thing — it had to happen. In spite of his hatred toward Devin, he knew that forgiveness had to take place in order for Rachel to move on. So he turned and walked away unseen so that a much needed reconciliation could take place in their lives. Things were about to really change.

# CHAPTER 38

## Devin's Judgment Day

Michael Stern sat in his chauffeur-driven, black limousine enjoying a peaceful ride to the courthouse. This was the day he had long waited for—a day of vindication. The peacefulness would not last long—he knew seeing Devin would bring up an anger that had been burning far too long in his heart. Wanting to lash out at the murderer of his one and only sister and picturing what he would do to his enemy haunted his mind daily.

In Michael's mind, the verdict had already been declared. Devin was guilty of murder and he would pay for his sin. Although there would not be a panel of jury members to hear the case, Michael felt some sense of relief that Devin would sit before a judge and two lawyers, putting him on Front Street to find out if there was a case to be settled. One way or the other, he would pay his debt to society in memory of Melinda.

Opening the window that separated him from his driver, he said, "Eli, how much longer before we get to our destination?"

"Five minutes, sir—only five minutes more."

"Good. Once we get there, you can go to the Parliament, sit down and eat lunch. I'll text you when I'm ready."

"Thank you, sir."

"Josh already knows you're coming so order whatever you'd like…he'll take care of you."

"That sounds right nice, sir. Thanks so much!"

Rounding the corner, they pulled up in front of the courthouse—an historical looking, gray stone building.

"Here we are, sir."

"No need for you to get out, Eli. Enjoy lunch. I'll see you in a bit."

"Yes, sir."

As the limousine pulled away, Michael made his way up the steep steps in front of the building. There was also a nicely dressed man in a gray, two-piece suit walking a few steps ahead of him up the concrete steps.

Opening the door, he graciously held the heavy, wooden door open as Michael entered.

"Thank you," said Michael.

"No problem," said the man as he continued on to his destination.

Each of their steps echoed on the ornate, mosaic stone floor of the corridor as they made their way to their separate destinations. The inquest was to begin soon. Michael would be meeting his lawyer in his office, which was located within the building, for their last meeting to confirm their plan of action.

As he walked through the office door, there was the smell of lavender coming from a diffuser that sat on the secretary's desk.

"Hi, Kierra...smells nice in here."

"Yes, I love it. The scent is so refreshing... also helps to relax me and everyone else," she said with a smile.

"Well, I may need a little of that," Michael said, pointing at the glass container.

"Attorney Grissom has been waiting for you. Go right in, Mr. Stern."

"Thanks!"

Walking through the open door of the office, Michael was greeted by his lawyer, James Grissom, Jr.

"Michael, thanks for coming in a little early. Have a seat, sir."

"Thanks, James. Let's cut to the chase—do you think we have a case here or not? I gave you a copy of Melinda's journals—what do you think?"

Shaking his head, he said, "Michael, like I told you before, it's going to be hard to produce a case against Mr. Vandelyn."

Jumping from his seat, Michael shouted, "No! I don't want to hear that? He was the cause of her death and I refuse to let him get away with it!"

"Michael! Please calm down! I didn't say that we wouldn't try. Just have a seat and listen to me. Here — have a glass of water."

"Don't patronize me," shouted Michael as he knocked the water away from himself spilling it onto the hard-wood floor.

Running into the office, Kierra said, "Is everything alright, Mr. Grissom?"

"Yes, Kierra — things are just fine. Please close the door on your way out."

"Yes, sir."

With a worried look on her face, Kierra walked out of the room mumbling, "I guess the lavender didn't work this time." She left the two of them alone, hoping there would be no more drama.

"Are you finished with your temper tantrum?" James asked, as he picked the glass up from the floor and placed it on his desk.

"You notice this glass didn't break? It was specially made for clients like you."

Michael looked up and could not help but laugh. Composing himself, he said, "I'm sorry, James, but it's been a stressful few months for me. Can we start all over?"

"Yes we can. Now like I was saying, before I was so abruptly interrupted, this is going to be a hard case. This is not our first discussion about this. The journals are good, but they are not good enough. We're going on hearsay evidence. It will be up to Devin to take owner-ship of what he did to cause her death. If and when he does, the judge may or may not even choose jail time for him. Are you ready to accept that fact?"

"No—I'm not. He has to pay in some way...he just has to."

"Then what's it going to take to satisfy you?"

Shaking his head, Michael said, "At this point, I real-ly don't know. I just pray that he sees the error of his ways and admits what he did to my sister. I won't be able to live with anything else. Something has to be done either way."

"I'm not sure what's going to be done Michael, but you're going to have to live with whatever happens in that courtroom. Let's just hope and pray that Devin admits to wrongdoing and that you'll be able to move on with your life when it's all said and done. And listen, you have to keep your temper in check—the judge may lock you up if you're not careful. Come on—we need to get moving or we'll be late."

James grabbed his briefcase and the two of them exit-ed his office. Kierra seemed relieved when she saw the two men walking out. Michael gently smiled at her as they left the office.

# CHAPTER 39

## The Decision of Culpability

Talking one last time about their strategy, Devin and his lawyer, Attorney Jessie Samuels, sat at a table adjacent to where his accuser would sit.

"Are you sure about this, Devin?"

"I'm sure...have to do it or I will never have any real peace of mind."

"Like I've told you before, they don't have a real case against you—it doesn't have to go this way."

"I know, but, at this time in my life, what you're saying really doesn't even matter. I have to take responsibility for what I did to cause her death and the death of our unborn child. I was a coward and I was evil to her. I regret every freaking minute of it," he said, cupping his head between his hands.

"Okay, but just know that I don't agree with what you're about to do."

"I know, but it's the only way I can do this—it's only right."

"Devin, just do one thing for me—let's hear what Judge Mathers has to say first. He's been looking over these papers that were submitted by Mr. Stern's lawyer and me. Let's first see what his ruling is before we make any kind of statements or take extreme measures—we shouldn't leap to any conclusions and get ourselves in a bind with the judge. I'm positive that this case will never go before any Grand Jury, so let's not get ahead of ourselves."

"Jessie, it really doesn't matter what he says, but I'll go along with you. Either way, I'm going to admit what I've done and apologize for my wrongdoing—I've got to do this."

As he was talking, Michael and his lawyer walked in. When Michael saw Devin and realized that he was the one who opened the door for him earlier, fire lit in his eyes and he said, "You are one lucky son of—"

"Michael! What did I tell you?"

His attorney knew that this was going to be a long session if Michael continued to show anger and speak out of turn.

Michael wouldn't let it go and said to Devin, "Had I known who you were, I would have flung you back down those concrete stairs and ended your life today!"

Holding him back, his lawyer said, "Come on, Michael. Have a seat."

Looking over at Devin, Michael's anger was unrelenting. Devin turned his face away and tried to compose the racing of his hard pounding heart. Unsettled nerves were causing palpitations in his chest.

Attorney Samuels could see that his client was struggling and poured him a glass of water. "Here, Devin—just relax."

Taking the tall, thin glass in his shaking hand, he looked at the floating ice and the condensation running down each side and said to himself, *I wish this was a glass of vodka on the rocks — I would drink it right down without taking a breath. I need something that will quickly calm my nerves.* Imagining it to be vodka, he held the glass tightly and quickly drank the water down. As he sat the glass onto the cherry wood table, he licked his lips as if trying to get the full intensity of his imaginary alcoholic drink.

As he came back to reality, Devin could feel hatred emanating from Michael's eyes, penetrating him like daggers. He tried his best to keep from looking in his direction. If Devin was able to trade seats with his lawyer, he would have done so expeditiously, but tradition kept him from doing so — the lawyer would have to sit on his right-hand side which put him in the direct sight of Michael Stern. There was no way he could avoid facing his nemesis.

Hearing the wise counsel of his lawyer was obliterated as questions danced within the crevices of Devin's mind...*How can I make amends with this guy? What am I supposed to do — God, please! You've got to turn things around? I've changed, so change this situation for me — please!*

He could hear the seriousness in Michael's voice as he spoke with his own lawyer. *His voice is so haunting – it sounds so familiar,* thought Devin. At that moment, a chill suddenly ran through his veins when a flashback occurred. He could no longer hear any conversation that came from the lips of his own lawyer. It was Michael's voice that got his attention, blocking out anything else that was occurring around him.

A gnawing, sickening feeling groveled in his belly as he grabbed a tissue and wiped his forehead. He became nauseous as he came to the realization of who his nemesis really was. The bruises that had healed long ago now ached within his body. A spasm in his rib cage almost caused him to fall over in his seat.

Concerned about his client, his lawyer asked, "Are you okay, Devin?"

"Not really – I'm just...can we get this over with?"

"It's not up to me. It'll be up to Judge Mathers."

Pouring himself another glass of water, he thought back to the night that he was brutally beaten in his own apartment by the masked stranger, who was now no longer a stranger, but was the one who sat accusing him in this courtroom. Fear gripped him as he pondered the fact that he was almost killed by this man who sat across from him, trying to put him away for good. *How am I going to be protected from this man who is trying to avenge the death of his sister? What culpability do I really have in this?*

Devin's thoughts were suddenly interrupted as they were asked to stand for the entrance of Judge Horace Mathers. Dressed in his black judicial robe with white trim, he entered and the room grew silent.

Judge Mathers was a short, salt and pepper-haired, balding man who made his first mark as a highly rated trial lawyer, winning ninety-five percent of his cases. He was now one of the state's top judges and was admired by most lawyers, and feared by others.

Quickly sitting down, he looked around as if expecting to see a full courtroom. He then set his eyes on Michael's lawyer and said, "I've been looking over your case file and asked myself, why in the universe this man would be disturbing my weekend with such frivolity?"

Michael breathed loudly and adjusted himself in his seat, wanting to defend the words that had come from Judge Mathers' lips. He thought better of it as he cringed within.

"You do know that I see no basis in continuing with this case, and would be a complete idiot if I were to allow you to take this to the Grand Jury."

"But, Judge, if you read the transcripts you can see from—"

Interrupting him, Judge Mathers said, "I read it and I am not impressed or convinced of anything, sir. This is a bunch of malarkey set in motion by a man who cannot and will not accept the fact that his little sister was unhappy with life and killed herself. You have a minute to prove me wrong."

With that, Judge Mathers looked firmly at Michael, who was now fired up with red hot anger. Devin feared for the judge's safety knowing what Michael was capable of. He knew that in some way, this was an opportune time and could be his moment of victory. He would try and make things better for all involved.

Getting the attention of his lawyer, he said, "I've got to do this—it's now or never."

"But, Devin..."

Not waiting for his response, Devin spoke up and said, "Judge, may I say something, please?"

"Is this going to help things or make them more frivolous than they already are? I'm not saying that you have a completely clean slate in this mockery, Mr. Vandelyn. You did cause this woman a lot of anguish and distress in her life with your meanness, but you did not put your hands on his sister and kill her. I'm warning you—don't make me regret giving you my time in this court. Now—what would you like to say?"

As Devin stood, his lawyer tried one last time to prevent him from committing what he thought was another suicide before Judge Mathers.

"Devin, you don't want to do this. Please think about the consequence?"

"I have to—I need to do this."

"Get on with it, young man," said the judge.

"Judge Mathers, lawyers, and Mr. Stern—since receiving the summons, the magnitude of how I treated Melinda and my culpability in her death have been strongest in my mind. Yes, Judge, I was mean and did some terrible things that I attest to and take full ownership of. At that time in my life, I was a drunken mess of a man, Judge, but I have since changed. The AA and the grace and mercy of God have been my secret companions. With the stress of being here, this day has been the only time within several months that I have given any kind of consideration to having a cold drink of vodka."

"Both you and I, son—you and I," said Judge Mathers with a chuckle.

"Judge, I admit that my actions were terrible in the way that I mistreated her, and I also admit that I may have caused her to feel like taking her own life. Standing here today, I feel that there is no way I can make amends to Mr. Stern, knowing that I can't bring Melinda back to life. But, Mr. Stern I know it was you who broke into my apartment and beat me half to death. You already started the process and have taken some revenge out on me."

The shock was revealed on Michael's face when he realized that Devin now knew that he was the one who had beaten him and stolen from his family.

Wanting to know more, Judge Mathers asked, "Just what are you talking about?"

"Judge, I'd rather not go into any details right now – we're not here for that...it's another matter. Like I said, I don't know how I can make amends — it's really up to Mr. Stern and the outcome he wants to see in this case. Judge, I just want it to be done and over with. I'm standing here to admit my guilt and that I was a mean, angry and heartless man in that lifetime. I did things to hurt Melinda and today it appalls me to even think about it. Back then, I didn't have the mentality to admit how crazy I was but, today, I stand before you a new man and accept the accusation. I am ready for my fate in this issue. I am guilty of the hurt and shame that I placed upon that beautiful woman whose life ended too soon."

"Hmm…" said Judge Mathers. Looking to Michael he said, "Mr. Stern, let me address you — since you have obviously already taken some matters into your own hands, which I am anxious to hear more about — what are you looking to get out of this case? What retribution are you asking for?"

Michael seemed dumbstruck. Knowing that his prior actions were no longer a secret and could potentially be made public, he needed a moment for counsel.

"Judge, can I please have a moment with my lawyer?"

"Yes. You have 10 minutes and you better make good use of it," said Judge Mathers as he stood up and left the courtroom.

As Devin sat down, his lawyer said, "Wow, Devin, you have really flipped the script here. What did he do to you?"

Explaining what happened and all he had gone through, Devin's lawyer now realized that this case was inevitably up to Michael Stern. How would he proceed knowing that he would have to reveal his culpability in what he had done to Devin and his family? A smirk appeared on Attorney Samuel's face as he turned to face Michael and his lawyer waiting for the judge to return.

Expecting that this case was over, Judge Mathers returned and was now dressed in casual clothing and ready for a day of leisure.

He settled in his chair and asked, "Okay, what do we have here? What are we doing to end this mockery?"

Standing, Michael's lawyer said, "Judge, first we apologize for bringing this case before you and would like to dismiss the charges."

"Hmm...I can't let you get off that easy. You wasted my time here today. Mr. Stern, are you really going to let things go? Or do you have some other plan already in that evil mind of yours?"

Michael lowered his head in embarrassment and the judge said, Now, Mr. Stern, let me make myself absolutely clear as I state the following. I want you to write this on the tablet of your heart today. If I hear of anything happening to this man — and I mean anything — if he even stubs his little toe and ends up in the hospital...sneezes and gets a bloody nose and has to go to the emergency room, I'm looking for you and you will serve time. Oh...that includes any member of his family too. Mr.

Stern, I want your word that you are through with the idea of vengeance. This is something that you have to make peace with. Your sister is dead! You have to move on and get a life! Do you understand me, sir? I'm waiting for an answer!"

Michael shook his head in agreement and the judge said, "That's not good enough. Look at me when I'm talking to you; open up your mouth and let me hear you, now! Do you understand everything I have said?"

Lifting his head and meeting Judge Mathers' eyes, he said, "Yes, Judge…I understand you."

Michael's demeanor had changed greatly. He knew that Judge Mathers was serious and it was no longer a matter that was in his own hands. He had a choice to make. He could either follow the orders or end up in jail. For Michael, jail time was not an alternative that he wanted to deal with, so he would choose to do as he was told.

Judge Mathers was not finished with Michael and said, "Now I want you to go over to Mr. Vandelyn and shake hands in agreement. When you do so, make sure you are sincere about it. Mark my words, fellow — you better be careful how you treat him and his family."

Michael was livid, but stood up and slowly made his way over to Devin. Already standing, Devin was ready. As they stood face to face, Devin put his hand out and said, "Mr. Stern, I am honestly sorry for everything. Please accept my apology."

Michael grimaced and with pierced lips said nothing as he tightly gripped Devin's hand. Feeling the pain permeate his entire being, Devin thought his bones would be broken, but didn't let on to the judge what he was happening.

"I'm warning you, Mr. Stern," said Judge Mathers. Heeding the judge, he slowly loosened his grip on Devin's hand—the pain subsided as Michael walked away.

Judge Mathers said, "Now listen, before you leave this building today, you are to get with both lawyers and sign a document of commitment, acknowledging all that I have set forth on this day. That commitment will be filed in this county courthouse for future reference. Do you understand me and what I am saying to you?"

Without hesitation, Michael said, "Yes, Judge. I understand clearly."

"Make sure you do. Attorney Grissom and Attorney Samuels, make sure there's a copy left on my desk no later than early Monday morning."

With those words, Judge Mathers banged his gavel and said, "Case dismissed. Have a blessed day, men." He quickly left them to their final business of getting the paperwork together.

# CHAPTER 40
## It's Over

Michael sat tapping the fingers of his right hand on the long, rectangular, wooden table in a conference room that was adjacent to Judge Mathers' chambers. Although he was angry about the outcome of the hearing, he could not help but feel some semblance of relief that it was now over — it had to be whether or not he agreed. Never being one who liked following strict rules and guidelines, this was now something he had to do; if not, he'd have to face the consequences handed down by the judge. There was no getting away this time.

Watching the two attorneys stand side by side next to the printer, laughing and joking with each other, did not help matters as he sat there impatiently waiting to sign the document of commitment. Ambivalence was having a field day in his mind as he thought about all the games he had played with the lives of others to get to where he was now. It was a pretty pathetic picture, but he thought he had every right to avenge his sisters' death.

Sitting there gave him a chance to calm down and think things over. *How awkward is this? I was trying to get Devin to pay, but somehow, I end up being the one executed. How did this happen? Who have I really become?* Thinking about this, he reached into his pocket and pulled out a stick of chewing gum. Once unwrapped, he folded it in half and placed the gum in his mouth. He then took the silver-colored piece of paper and scrunched it up until it became a tiny ball. Rolling it back and forth from hand to hand, he thought about his dilemma if Devin were to ever reveal his beating and how he had robbed them of the valuable jewelry. *Wow...It's a good thing I at least returned that jewelry when I did. I could really be in a world of trouble. Hope he never opens his mouth.*

A feeling of genuine sadness overtook him as he thought, *And his aunt didn't even have to die! That didn't have to happen, but it did. I wasn't there, but I'm still to blame.* He sighed deeply.

Michael was now more agitated than ever and banged his fist on the table shouting, "What's taking so long?" Surprised by Michael's aggressive behavior, his attorney looked over and said, "It's almost done. Just a few more pages need to be printed."

Shaking his head, Michael responded, "What are you doing...publishing a book? I need to get out of here. I've got business to attend to."

"Just have patience. You'll be able to leave soon enough," said Attorney Samuels.

Thoughts ran deep within as Michael thought about Melinda and how she would feel about all that had transpired. *I don't think she'd be too pleased with me right about now.* His eyes began to glisten as tears gathered at the base of his eyes and he quickly wiped them away before anyone could see the drops begin to roll down his face.

It was just in time. When he removed his hand, both attorneys were standing there. Attorney Samuels had the document in hand and laid it before him.

"The first twenty pages need to be initialed and then sign, print your name, and date the last page," he said. Michael quickly picked it up, flipped through the pages and said, "Does anyone have a pen?"

Before releasing the pen to his client, Attorney Grissom said, "Don't you want to read it first?"

"No, I'm good...the judge said it all." Michael, took the pen and quickly scribbled his initials and then his signature as requested.

"Put a copy in the mail," he said as he stood to leave and handed the pen back to his lawyer. Walking down the empty hallway, he prayed that the loud echo of his footsteps would drown out the guilt that was resonating within the very core of his being. He knew that things had to change and now was the time...he had no choice.

His life had been obsessed with getting revenge on Devin, causing him to lose sight of who he really was. Yes, Jess and he had done some criminal-like things, but nothing could ever compare to this stint. He felt ashamed and embarrassed.

# CHAPTER 41
## Reconciled Differences

D evin couldn't wait to see Rachel. *I have to get to her and tell her it's over — Rachel, it's all over.* These words resonated repeatedly in his head as he left the courthouse. A sense of relief overwhelmed him and tears filled his eyes.

Before this day of revelation, there were many long, sleepless nights. *Tonight, I'll be able to rest peacefully and not worry and think about any of this again. I have a great future ahead of me and I won't let my dark past stop me from being successful,* he thought, as he walked to the end of the corridor.

He took a deep breath of fresh air as it hit his face exiting the building and then walked to the west side of the parking lot. His footsteps crunched on the gravel, when suddenly he heard a second set of steps and stood face to face with Michael Stern. Happy thoughts were short-lived and fear filled him looking into the face of the one who had made him an archenemy. Devin tried to get past him, but Michael blocked his way refusing to let him move any further.

"Mr. Stern, I'm sure you are well aware that you're about to be in violation of your commitment to the court?"

Michael didn't say a word—he just stood there with a certain boldness that put fear in the heart of Devin, whose mind was on nothing but finding an escape route. Michael then stepped back and slowly pulled his hand out of his pocket, startling Devin, who was just about to make a run for it. Devin stopped in place when he realized that Michael was extending a weaponless hand, saying, "I accept your apology." He then waited for Devin to respond by accepting his outstretched hand.

Devin, being caught off guard and fearful of this man who stood before him, nervously said, "What did you say?"

"I said, I accept your apology and also ask you to forgive me for what I did to you and your family. It was the work of a man who was angry and set on getting his way. It was hard for me to accept the fact that my sister took her own life. I wanted someone to blame so I took it all out on you, especially when I began reading her journals. Judge Mathers opened my eyes today and helped me to see exactly what I needed to see about me and this demon that has possessed me for a long time. It made me angry."

Devin had a hard time believing what he was hearing and stood there for a moment, trying to process what Michael was saying.

"Oh, and I'm sorry about getting that last squeeze in," said Michael with a slight grin.

Devin looked down at his hand, wiggling his fingers, he said, "I can move them—nothing broken."

Michael went on to say, "Even with the issues and the way you treated her, my sister loved you Devin. It's time for me to deal with these feelings."

The fear that had gripped Devin slowly dissipated as his trembling hand reached out and he said, "Thanks, Mr. Stern."

Shaking hands, the once angry accuser said, "Please call me Michael; I'm not that much older than you, Devin. Now I'm not saying this is going to be an easy road of forgiveness, but if I keep saying it and let my mind hear it, I know that I will finally be totally free of the feelings of anguish and hurt. The judge was right, I need to let go of this and get on with my life."

Finally feeling relaxed, Devin shook his head in agreement and said, "I understand. Thanks, this really means a lot to me."

Walking slowly to his waiting limousine, Michael stopped, turned back to Devin and said, "Hey, my chef makes the best lobster and steak dish. Are you up for it?"

"I could use a good meal right now, but I'd like to first call my sister."

"Bring her with you."

"Thanks, Michael. Where should we meet?"

"At the Parliament."

"Once I tell her the good news, I'm sure she'd love to meet you."

Smiling and shaking his head, Michael said, "Oh — we've met."

"Really," said Devin with a hint of curiosity. "And just how did that happen," he asked.

"Well, let me tell you," said Michael.

Walking together, new friendships were now on the horizon as Michael shared how he met Rachel and thanked God that an INTRUSION intercepted his evil schemes.

# THE EPILOGUE

Michael Stern sat in his den thinking about the events that had occupied his day. Sitting at his desk, he laid out his sister Melinda's journals in front of him. "It's time to let them go," he sadly said. Standing, he gathered each one, walked over to the fireplace which was started the moment he walked into the room, and he began slowly throwing each one into the blazing fire. Although tears were flowing down his face, peacefulness permeated his heart.

Holding the last journal that had been marked by her tears, he stopped and held it to his heart and said, "It's over, I have to let you go, Melinda. I'll always love you and will never forget you." With that, he kissed the journal and then threw it into the flames. For the longest, he stood there and watched the fury of red flames, as they burned the journals until there were nothing but ashes. No more hurt, sorrow or pain was left for him to revisit. It was time to leave the past and move on to the future. How could he now build a positive memorial and bury the negative past? It would be a challenge, but he was ready to do it.

He went back to his desk to sit down, wiped away his tears and thought about his dinner with the Vandelyns. At first it was a little stressful. When Rachel recognized him, he could see fear written on her face. Devin was able to calm her shaken nerves.

Before placing their orders, Michael sat down with them and apologized profusely for all he had done. He tried to explain everything and made no excuses for what he did. A new day had dawned and life was heading in a better direction. He was now free from the turmoil of his obsession with trying to get revenge.

Even with the apologies, there were mixed emotions. Rachel was still a little hesitant and slow to forgive. Knowing that Michael Stern was partially to blame for Aunt Myra's death, she left the restaurant questioning whether or not he should get away with what he had done.

Devin tried his best to convince her that everyone needed to go on with life and just let the past go. He even quoted a scripture from Romans which says, "Don't insist on getting even; that's not for you to do. I'll do the judging," says God. "I'll take care of it." At first when he said it, she tried ignoring him, but conviction tugged at her heart and she could not forget those word, especially since it was the word of God and coming from Devin's lips. It was something unimaginable; he had really changed for the better.

Before going to bed that night, Devin got down on his knees and prayed a prayer of thanksgiving and praise to God for all that He had done in his life. He was no longer the same nasty, hateful and arrogant person he once was and it felt good to live a more righteous life. Devin knew that he still had a long way to go, but he was on the road to a life worth living. There was a God and he was now a believer. He had a lot of making up to do with family and friends and knew that it would take a great work on his part. Patience and God's direction would have to be at the forefront of reconciliation and getting them to trust him.

Trevor also made a turn for the better and was slowly developing a relationship with Devin. Hearing his apology to Rachel helped to fan the flame that caused him to see the sincerity of heart in Devin. Rachel was the love of his life and he knew that in order for her to forgive and see her brother in a new light, he would also have to be accepting of Devin.

An *intrusion* caused an interruption in the lives of these persons. In order to get past the hurt and pain that is often felt in any *intrusion*, choices have to be made. You can either live with the *intrusion*, making it a part of your everyday life or make the choice to release it by letting go of the pain and hurt that's been caused by an *intrusion*. It's up to you as to whether or not you will hold on to it, or let it go and see how God can handle that *intrusion* of life.

Remember, God is always in the midst of your sorrows. He will close the door on that intrusion. Just take a stance, that's all you have to do, and let God have His way!

## The End

# ABOUT THE AUTHOR

Theresa is an accomplished writer and has written several plays, which include "The Gift", "Murder at the Reunion", "Baal's Revenge", the dramatic presentation of "Born to Die" and has also written several skits entitled the "Conference Room" that were used for altar call presentations at her former church. Her first published book is a non-fiction entitled "My Life Tested: Earthly vs. Spiritual Things", and her first fiction novel is titled, "Jalena Dances with God". Both can be purchased on Amazon. Intrusion is her first try at writing dramatic, mystery fiction.

Today, in addition to writing, her focus is on singing, songwriting, presenting and writing dramatic plays with DMO Music and Creative Arts. This organization is named after her mother, Delila Melrose Odom. Her heart's desire is to touch the lives of people creatively, in song, writing and drama.

On September 17, 1995, Theresa was licensed and ordained as a minister of the Gospel of Jesus Christ. Today she is an active member, and leader at Empire Christian Center, under the leadership of Pastors Tre and Christina Staton.

www.ingramcontent.com/pod-product-compliance
Lightning Source LLC
Chambersburg PA
CBHW070332260626
47160CB00003B/1025